A

One of the troopers started sprinting toward a corner of the house. Suddenly a gigantic figure loomed out of the shadow of a bush. Klute! Raider realized. And he was carrying a sawed-off double-barreled shotgun. The trooper tried to bring up his rifle, but Klute let him have one barrel. The load of buckshot hammered the trooper backward, lifting him off his feet. And now the barrels were tracking onto Raider. "You son-of-a-bitch!" Klute screamed, but by then Raider had his rifle to his shoulder, and his first bullet took Klute high in the left shoulder, spoiling his aim. The load of shot tore splinters from the side of the building next to Raider's head . . .

J.D. HARDEN

COLORADO
SILVER QUEEN

BERKLEY BOOKS, NEW YORK

COLORADO SILVER QUEEN

A Berkley Book/published by arrangement with
the author

PRINTING HISTORY
Berkley edition/January 1985

ISBN: 0-425-07386-6

A BERKLEY BOOK® TM 757,375
Berkley Books are published by The Berkley Publishing Group,
200 Madison Avenue, New York, N.Y. 10016.
The name "BERKLEY" and the stylized "B" with design are trademarks
belonging to Berkley Publishing Corporation.

CHAPTER ONE

Doc was dressing himself with his usual meticulous care, knotting his foulard silk tie, critically eyeing himself all the while in the big mirror that topped the immense walnut dresser at one end of his hotel room. Tonight he had chosen an ensemble in gray: pearl gray silk vest; soft gray cambric shirt; a suit of the finest English wool, the jacket not on yet; patent leather shoes with genuine mother-of-pearl buttons; a gray derby hat still hanging rakishly from a chair back. "Damn," Doc muttered as he struggled with the straps of his shoulder holster. He finally got it just right, not too tight, then settled his modishly cut suit jacket into place. He was admiring the effect in the mirror when he suddenly saw movement behind him—a door opening. Doc's hand instantly dropped to the pistol lying on the dresser top. "Oh, it's you, Raider," he said, turning, holding the pistol down at his side.

Raider closed the interconnecting door from his own adjoining room and stood looking at his partner. "If you don't take the cake as dude o' the century!" he said, grinning at Doc's sartorial splendor.

"I'd take that as a compliment," Doc replied acidly, "if it weren't for the source."

Raider definitely represented a completely different school of fashion, sporting well-worn jeans, calfskin Middleton boots, a denim shirt, and a worn leather jacket, the whole topped by a disreputable battered Stetson that had seen many, many years of hard service. However, the attire suited Raider. He was a big man, much bigger than Doc, wide-shouldered, sun-bronzed, his drooping black mustache screening white teeth that set off a lean, rangy face. "I see you bought one o' them newfangled Colts," he said to Doc.

"I certainly didn't steal it," Doc replied, hefting the pistol. He held it out to Raider. "Double-action."

"Don't see why that's so all-fired important," Raider murmured as he turned the revolver over in his hand.

"It cocks itself when you pull the trigger." Taking the pistol back, Doc quickly shucked out the cartridges, then pulled the trigger several times. Raider watched as the hammer repeatedly moved itself back to full cock, then fell. "Spooky," he said. "Like there was an invisible thumb."

"Ah, you've been practicing English again," Doc said, aiming the pistol and clicking the action in the direction of his image in the mirror. "This easily doubles the pistol's rate of fire, Raider."

Raider, somewhat stung by Doc's comment about his vocabulary, snapped, "Ain't speed that counts. What counts is where you put the bullet—how cool a man can keep himself."

"True, but all other things equal, this could be a life-saver."

"Maybe," Raider agreed somewhat reluctantly. Then he took a closer look at the pistol. "Ah, gee, Doc, when you gonna learn? You bought the *Lightning*. It's only thirty-eight caliber."

"Still preaching your cannon gospel?" Doc drawled. "Yes, I could have bought the Thunderer in a heavier caliber. But it's too big a piece. It would ruin the line of my jacket."

Raider sighed. "It sure does beat that thirty-two-caliber popgun you used to carry," he admitted. "Hell, I remember the time that squirrel threw that little bitty bullet right back at you."

Raider himself wore on his right hip, in a well-oiled holster, a Model 1875 Remington single-action revolver, in caliber .44-.40, which packed nearly twice the wallop of Doc's streamlined little revolver. He watched his partner reload the pistol and settle it into its shoulder holster. Doc adjusted his jacket a couple of times and at last seemed satisfied. "You steppin' out?" Raider asked casually.

"Yes. Down to the Calle de los Negros, to teach some of the locals the laws of chance."

"You playin' poker in Nigger Alley again?"

Doc stared icily at Raider. "I don't like that word, Raider. I fought in a war to get rid of words like that."

"Don't get on your high horse," Raider flared back. "I fought in the same war . . . to keep blue-black Yankees like you from rapin' our women and stealin' our land."

Doc stood with his feet wide apart, his face unreadable, but Raider could tell he'd been stung, because he produced one of his evil-smelling little cheroots from an inside pocket and proceeded with great deliberation to light it. Once he had it lit, he inhaled, then blew a stream of acrid smoke in Raider's direction. Raider hated the smell of those cigars, and Doc knew it. "See you around, Johnny Reb," he said softly, then turned and started toward the door.

"Hey, hold on," Raider called after the smaller man. "You ain't answered the question I asked you last night. What the hell are we doin' here in this fancy dump?"

Doc turned, exhaling another stream of smoke. "Why, enjoying ourselves in the midst of the best local attempt at civilized luxury."

Raider looked around at the well-appointed room. "Hell, who needs it?" he snorted. "We should be keepin' in touch with the Denver office, lettin' 'em know where the hell we are. Shit, Doc, you ain't even filed a daily report for more'n two weeks."

Doc's mouth gaped in delighted astonishment, and he

bent over, hooting with laughter. "You...you..." he stammered, pointing the cigar at Raider. *"You're* telling *me* I should be filing my daily reports?"

Raider flushed. "Well, hell, Doc, I know I ain't been real strong on that in the past, but you... Hell, this ain't like you—lettin' everything go, holin' up in this fancy hotel, spendin' money like water, and worst of all, waltzin' off every night to play cards with hardcases worse'n half the hombres we've hauled in so's they could hang 'em."

Doc stopped laughing. "My friend," he said solemnly, "there are more ways to punish the lawless than the simple-minded expedient of the rope. I've decided to apply to these hardcases you mentioned, something... shall we call it a little *economic* castigation. In short, I have decided to play the part of a modern Robin Hood, using the medium of the painted pasteboard to take from the thief his ill-gotten gains and redistribute them to the truly deserving—namely, myself."

Raider's face screwed up with effort as he tried to decipher his partner's words. "I guess you mean playin' cards," he said hesitantly.

"Give the man a cigar," Doc said, holding out the one smoldering in his hand. Then, seeing the look of disgust on Raider's face, he prudently withdrew the hand. He was well aware that there was a point beyond which he should not goad his partner. Not without a high probability of grievous bodily harm. He had a missing tooth to testify to that, or rather, a gold crown, generously supplied by a repentant Raider.

"Hey, you ain't cheatin' them boys, are you, Doc?" Raider asked worriedly. "'Cause they're meaner'n a nest full o' stepped-on rattlers."

Doc snorted derisively. "Cheat? What do you take me for, a bungler? One doesn't waste energy by cheating animals of the low mental capacities of my esteemed gambling partners. Their crass stupidity and childish braggadacio are enough in themselves to set the money rolling in my direction, like a manifestation of the immutable laws of the universe. Now, goodbye, Raider. I don't want to be late for the night's fleecing."

Doc set his derby jauntily on his well-brushed head, then turned and walked from the room, leaving Raider standing flat-footed, staring concernedly after his partner. Without a backward glance, Doc closed the door and set off down the hall toward the stairway. His room, and Raider's next to it, were on the second floor of the hotel. Gas lamps in the hallway imparted a soft golden glow to the expensive wood-work. Not a bad hotel, Doc thought. Hot water even on the upper floors. Yes, this town might have possibilities . . . given another forty or fifty years.

The sun was just going down when Doc stepped out into a balmy Los Angeles evening. He took a moment to admire the old Spanish plaza that was still the heart of the little city. True, large modern buildings of several stories were now in evidence, but the old Spanish church with its unusual gazebo-style bell tower and a scattering of long low adobes with tile roofs imparted a quaint charm. Doc turned and looked back at the Pico House, from which he had just exited, without a doubt the finest hotel in Los Angeles. Three stories high. A few blocks away he heard a horse-drawn streetcar rumbling by. Yes, the underpinnings of civilization, but still no match for the old established culture of his native Boston.

As Doc walked across the plaza, a large oval ringed by low trees and bushes, he noticed a man sauntering by car-rying a rifle. No, definitely not quite civilized. Not yet.

His destination lay only a short distance away—La Calle de los Negros. The Street of the Blacks. It had been called that, by the Spanish, because of the large number of darker-skinned people—Indians and mestizos, people of mixed blood, who lived there. When the Americans had arrived, they had translated the name literally, thus its ap-pellation by the ignorant, Doc reflected, as Nigger Alley.

The Street of the Blacks was also Los Angeles's China-town. Doc had been told that only a few years before, in 1871, a white mob had lynched over twenty Chinese on the suspicion that one of them *might* have killed a white man.

At the present time the area comprised Los Angeles's saloon and red-light district. It was not a pretty area: low crumbling adobes, peeling paint—where there was any paint; a drunk lying sprawled half off the sagging boardwalk. Doc fastidiously flicked an imaginary speck of dust from his jacket as he stepped onto the boardwalk and headed for his destination, a small, evil-smelling card room and saloon. It was not a place that advertised itself. He had to knock loudly on a heavy door. It was opened by a wizened little man who scrutinized Doc for several seconds before he let him in.

"Well, if it ain't the dude," a loud voice said as Doc stepped into a room about twenty feet square, lit by several kerosene lamps with, as Doc noted, grimy chimneys. There was one large round table in the center of the room, with several men seated at it. Half of them were Mexicans, but hardly the same sort of Mexican as California's former governor, Pio Pico, who just a few years before had built the plush Pico House. These were hard men, apparently up from south of the border. Bandits, Doc thought, taking in their wide-brimmed sombreros, drooping mustaches, crossed gunbelts, and hard, hard eyes.

Then there were the Anglos, the Bates brothers, three big, sloppily dressed, gun-hung hardcases who showed their relationship principally in their close-set, piggish little eyes.

It was Jake Bates who had greeted Doc. He waved to an empty chair halfway around the table from himself and his two brothers. "Set yourself down awhile, dude," he said in his loud, coarse voice, "an' git plucked like a chicken."

His two brothers, who usually followed Jake's lead, snickered noisily. Doc coolly looked over the three men. "I recall walking out of here yesterday with all my feathers and a great deal of plumage previously belonging to you," he said evenly to Jake as he took the proffered seat.

Jake's mean little eyes narrowed even further, if possible, causing Doc to wonder if men like Jake might have been responsible for the old myths about the cyclops. "You got me drunk," Jake snarled. "Won't happen tonight."

Doc looked at the half-empty bottle of cheap whiskey next to the glass in Jake's hand and he smiled. "What will it be, gentlemen?" he said quietly. "Draw or stud?"

It was stud, varying between seven and five card. The men sitting around the table, there were seven—three Mexicans, the three Bates brothers, and Doc—settled down to hard, concentrated play. For just a moment Doc savored the possibly lucky aspect of being the seventh man, but he quickly discarded it in favor of concentrating on the scientific application of the laws of chance. He carefully catalogued in his mind the cards as they were dealt one by one. During most of the game he was fairly certain what cards his opponents did and did not have.

Doc won steadily. Bit by bit the money showing on the table, most of it in gold and silver coins, moved into place in front of him. Only one other man, a Mexican named Gonzalez, had anything to show for his play. That's the man to watch, Doc thought.

The more he lost, the more agitated Jake Bates became. He began to talk too much, handling his cards jerkily. His brothers watched his every move, their hostility drifting toward Doc. Relishing this, Doc began to use it, insulting the Bateses, but in such a way, using such language, that they could not be certain, but only suspect that they were being made fun of. Correspondingly, the quality of their play deteriorated even further, sending more money Doc's way. The tension around the table grew progressively, the Mexicans playing with hooded eyes hidden in passive, half-Indian faces, the three Bateses becoming more and more frustrated and hiding it badly, and Doc, cool, urbane, unruffled, raking in pot after pot.

The showdown came on a big hand. The game was five-card stud, Doc dealing. Doc had nothing in the hole worth considering, but dealt himself a king face up for his fourth card. The betting was lively. Within a short time there was a glittering pile in the center of the table. Gonzalez had a queen showing. Jake Bates had an ace. Doc passed the cards around again. Gonzalez got his queen and Jake got another ace, which caused him to crow jubilantly until Doc dealt himself a second king. A tight situation. Three pairs showing.

Everyone else dropped out except Gonzalez, Doc, and Jake. "Your bet," Doc said to Jake, who was seated to his right. Jake hesitated. He had the high pair showing, but there was always the possibility that Doc might have another king in the hole. And was Gonzalez holding a hidden queen? "Forty bucks," Jake growled, pitching two gold double eagles into the pot.

The bet was around to Gonzalez now. He paid no attention at all to Jake, but looked long and hard into Doc's eyes. For the first time Doc felt uneasy. The Bateses were a noisy problem, but Gonzalez was genuinely dangerous.

To Doc's relief, Gonzalez tossed in his cards, then leaned back in his chair to watch the play. Doc made a small production of peeking at his hole card. "I'll see your twenty," he said quietly, "and raise you fifty." Looking Jake straight in the eye he added, "That is, if you have the stomach for it."

Jake's liquor-blotched face turned an even deeper shade of purple. "Why, you dandied-up little shit," he snarled.

"Are you playing with words or with money?" Doc snapped. "Call me or fold your hand."

Jake sat glaring at Doc, but still he didn't bet. Doc knew that Jake, like everyone else at the table, was growing more and more certain that Doc must have that third king in the hole. The younger of the Bates brothers verbalized this belief. "Careful, Jake," he muttered. "The son of a bitch just might have it. After all, he *is* dealing."

Jake's continuing hesitation convinced Doc that those two aces were his total hand. He glanced coolly at the younger Bates. "Are you intimating that I'm cheating?" he asked icily. There were three of the Bateses, but this one backed down. "I di'n't mean nothin'," he muttered sulkily.

Now Doc turned back to Jake. "And what do *you* mean?" he demanded, his voice whip-sharp. "Have you got fifty dollars worth of guts or not?"

Fifty dollars was about all that Jake had left in front of him. He picked up the money—two double eagles and a ten-dollar gold piece—and clenched it tightly in his fist, his eyes shifting back and forth between Doc and his two kings lying face up. "Ah, shit," he snarled. "Ain't no use throwin' good money after bad." And he threw in his hand.

Doc raked the pile of gold and silver toward him. Then, smiling slightly, he picked up his cards and, holding them in his hand, the hole card still hidden, faced Jake. "I'm going to let you see what fifty dollars worth of courage would have done for you," he said and, turning his cards over, showed the whole table how he had bluffed Jake Bates.

The reaction was a little more than Doc had bargained for. Jake lunged to his feet, his piggish eyes a blaze of red. "You stinkin', cheatin', duded-up little asshole," he snarled. "I'm gonna cash in your chips for good."

Jake was already reaching for the big .45 Peacemaker he wore low on one hip before Doc was certain the big man actually meant to kill him. He hadn't believed Bates would have enough guts, but here it comes, he thought, reaching for his own pistol in its hidden shoulder rig. He was late, of course—very, very late in drawing. He saw the .45 coming up, noticed how huge the hole in the end of the muzzle looked. Maybe Raider had a point about large calibers.

Doc's gun was in his hand now, and he remembered he didn't have to cock it. Jake's thumb was already pulling back the hammer on his single-action Colt when Doc jerked the trigger, trying for dead center on Jake but knowing even as his gun went off that that hasty tug on the trigger had thrown his aim askew. He was going to miss.

He did miss, but not in the way he expected. His .38 Lightning, firing more quickly than Jake's older pistol, sent its bullet low and to the left, neatly taking off Jake's right thumb. Jake never finished cocking his piece; it remained on half-cock with Jake frantically working the bloody stump of his thumb, not fully aware of what had happened.

But Doc was not yet out of the woods. He sensed movement all around him. Hostile movement. Jake still had a gun in his hands, and his brothers, howling angrily, were going for theirs. And to his left, where Gonzalez was, Doc caught the flash of bright steel. A knife. And he knew that no matter which target he picked next, he'd never be able to get all of them before they got him.

CHAPTER TWO

After Doc left, Raider nervously paced the hotel room. He was worried, had been worried for some time—worried about Doc. His partner was acting strangely, completely out of character. Doc was usually a stickler for going by the book, the Pinkerton National Detective Agency book, the organization for which they both worked. "The little bastard's gone clean out of his skull," Raider muttered. "Don't turn in his reports. Hell, won't even report in. That ain't *like* him."

Far more worrisome was the gambling and the company Doc was keeping. He was acting a damn sight as bad as some of the men they were hired to hunt down. More than once Raider had wanted to drop the whole thing, just let Doc drift along on his way into trouble, but he couldn't. As much of a pain in the ass as the little bastard was, with his high-falutin ways and his fancy duds and his god-awful cigars, he was still Raider's partner. They'd been through thick and thin together. So Raider had tagged along, from San Francisco, down through California's Central Valley,

11

and now to Los Angeles. And wherever they went, Doc managed to find a card game and a bunch of hardcases to fleece. He sure as hell knew how to win at cards, and he wasn't a cheapskate. He insisted on sharing all his winnings with Raider, but that kind of money made Raider nervous.

After a half hour of fruitless worrying, Raider left the hotel to look for something to eat. Although his pockets were jingling with money—an infrequent state of affairs for Raider—habit guided the big detective into a small, shabby place just off the plaza. It was run by an old Mexican couple, Papa playing waiter, Mama wedged in behind a tiny stove at one end of the room, fat and stocky from too much beans and rice, sweating like a miner working at the bottom of a three-thousand-foot shaft from the heat of her cooking. "Whatcha got?" Raider asked.

Sifting through the man's mixture of Spanish and English, Raider managed to pick out some familiar words. "Okay, some tamales and enchiladas," he said. "But don't make 'em too hot. You understand? *No picante.*"

Raider's touchy stomach was not a great fan of Mexican food, but he was already sitting down and he'd ordered and he'd be damned if he'd move. The food came quickly, a big plate heaped high with steaming hot food. The smell was delicious, reminding him how hungry he was. Throwing caution to the winds, Raider began gulping the tamales down, which was a mistake. The outer shell of corn *masa* masked the fiery spices inside just long enough for him to swallow a couple of times and to spoon more into his mouth.

From a modest beginning the fire grew into frightening proportions. Raider stopped chewing. His eyes bulged. "Water! Bring me water!" he managed to gasp around his mouthful of molten food.

The old man, rich in past experiences with gringos, already had the water waiting. Raider gulped it down, quenching the flames. "Aaaahhhh," he sighed, then saw that the old woman was grinning at him, Eyes watering, he bravely grinned back, and just to prove he was all man, he started eating again, but more slowly, and to his surprise he discovered that the food tasted as good as it smelled. He ordered a beer and, with its help, finished the meal. The hot spices imparted a completely different taste to the beer, and, in addition, the spices themselves gave him a rush of good feeling, so that by the time he walked outside, he was on top of the world. For once his stomach wasn't hurting. Maybe there was something to this Mexican food.

Without really deciding to do so, Raider let his feet drift in the direction of Nigger Alley. Uh-uh. Doc had a point. The Street of the Blacks. But where was the little bastard? Raider walked in and out of seedy bars and gambling joints, but no Doc. He finally decided to ask around. He'd noticed one man, a stocky, not-too-clean individual, moving from bar to bar, just like himself, and from the load he had on, Raider figured the man must have been doing it for quite a while. So he stopped the man and, after describing Doc, asked if he had seen him. The man looked up at him with mean, watery eyes. "What the hell's it to you, big-mouth?" he sneered.

Raider said nothing for a moment, just stood looking down at the man, who was a good head shorter, wearing a pistol at his belt, standing hip-shot like a dude's idea of a gunfighter from a Ned Buntline novel. Raider smiled and, reaching out, took hold of the man's chest. Not his shirt, but his chest, picking him up by his skin. "I asked you a question, shit-face," Raider said, still smiling pleasantly.

The man shrieked, clawing at Raider's hands, trying to break loose from that excruciating grip. Raider casually tossed him back against a wooden wall. The man bounced once, then stood panting heavily, pawing at the mauled skin of his chest. "I asked you once, real nice-like, if you'd seen my partner," Raider said quietly. "Now I'm askin' you again."

The man seemed to notice for the first time the well-worn butt of the .44 protruding from Raider's holster. "Yeah . . . yeah, I saw somebody like that," he said quickly, also noticing the look in Raider's eyes. The man pointed to a wooden door across the street. "He's probably in there. Goes in there a lot."

"Thank ya kindly for the help, stranger," Raider said.

"Now, why don't you go find yourself a drink somewhere."

The man nodded jerkily, then turned and half ran toward the nearest saloon. Raider watched him until he was out of sight. He wasn't chancing any back-shooting. Damn! He was getting all worked up.

Raider was halfway to the wooden door, determined to give Doc a piece of his mind, when a shot rang out from inside. "Oh hell," he swore and, drawing his .44, sprinted toward the door. With all his weight behind it, one kick drove the door inward, taking it completely off its hinges. The door flew into the room and collided with the second of the Bates brothers, breaking up the action just long enough for Raider to size up what was happening. "Don't try it, old son," he warned the youngest Bates, who had his gun half out of its holster. Staring into the cavernous muzzle of Raider's Remington, the young gunman prudently dropped his pistol onto the table. "Look out, Doc," Raider shouted. "The Mex's got a knife."

But Doc had already pinned Gonzalez's knife arm with his left hand, and, turning, he smashed him across the face with his pistol barrel. Gonzalez let go of the knife and reeled back, pressing both hands against the sudden spurt of blood above his cheekbone.

Doc backed away quickly, his pistol covering Jake Bates. "Drop it," he told Jake, "or my next bullet goes straight into your gut."

To emphasize his words, Doc cocked his .38. Jake had by now figured out why his pistol wouldn't cock. Of course, he could always reach up with his other hand and pull the hammer back, but Doc's pistol was pointed unwaveringly at his stomach. Jake let his pistol drop and pressed the bloody stump of his thumb against his shirt. "You son of a bitch," he snarled, his face twisted with hate. "I'll get you for this if it's the last thing I do."

"Is that so?" Doc answered in an amused voice. "Then maybe I'd better kill you now and save myself future grief."

Doc aligned his sights at a point directly between Jake's eyes. Jake paled, but the hate remained on his face.

"Doc!" Raider called out sharply.

Doc turned and gave his partner a crooked grin. "Just trying to save the state a little money," he said cheerfully. "They're going to have to hang him someday, you know."

"Shut up," Raider snarled. "Cover me."

He went from man to man, disarming first the Bates brothers, then the Mexicans. A considerable pile of hardware stacked up on the table: knives, revolvers, and two derringers.

"My goodness," Doc said, eyeing the weapons. "Paranoia seems to run rampant among you gentlemen."

Doc glanced at Gonzalez, who was standing quietly against the wall, blood running down his face. His eyes had been tracking Doc relentlessly. "You aren't going to forget, are you?" Doc asked the Mexican.

"No, señor," Gonzalez said quietly, his eyes boring into Doc's.

Doc sighed. "I thought not." He turned to Raider. "We'll lock them in the back room," he said, pointing to a heavy door set into one wall.

Raider nodded and herded the men into the room after making certain there were no weapons inside. Then he shut the door and dropped a heavy wooden bar into place. "That should give us about an hour," he said grimly to Doc.

"For what?"

"To get the hell out of here. We're gonna have a pack o' real upset hardcases on our trail just as soon as they get that door open."

Doc nodded. "Unbeatable logic. I'll be with you in a moment."

Going over to the table, Doc scooped up his winnings and poured them into his pockets, scrupulously taking only what was his. There were so many gold coins that Doc literally jingled as he walked out the door ahead of Raider. Fortunately, the old man who'd let him in had apparently vanished as soon as trouble had started. Doc hoped he hadn't gone for help.

Raider stopped off at the livery stable to order their horses bridled and saddled, while Doc went to the Pico House to collect their gear. It took only a few minutes to pack his saddlebags and sweep up Raider's bedroll, which was always kept ready for a quick move. Pausing downstairs at the desk, Doc quickly settled the bill, then went out into the street. Raider was already cantering into view with the horses. Another couple of minutes and the saddlebags and rifles were in place and Raider's bedroll lashed behind his saddle. They rode out, heading north toward the dark bulk of the hills marking the pass that led over into the San Fernando Valley.

"Good idea," Doc told Raider. "They'll think we're going north."

"Hell, we *are* going north. To the train at San Fernando."

"Just what they figure we'll do," Doc insisted. "We'll cut around town and head south down the riverbed. It's pretty dry this time of year."

"Hell, Doc, I don't *want* to go south," Raider snapped.

"Well, I do."

"What the hell for?"

"Why, to see San Diego, of course. I hear it's an interesting place. And, of course, to save my neck from Gonzalez and that ignorant ape, Bates. I hate to say it, but Gonzalez has the appearance of a man who bears a grudge. No sense of humor at all. None of them are going to rest until they've killed us both."

"Oh, great. Just great," Raider groaned. But he followed Doc when he turned his horse to the south.

CHAPTER THREE

They rode for a while alongside one of the old *zanjas,* the irrigation ditches the Spanish had built many years earlier. The moon was out; it was a clear night, warm and dry. Behind them were the mountains, ahead the flat Los Angeles plain. At the end of the *zanja* they picked up the riverbed and began following it south. The riverbed was mostly sand, since it was now three-quarters of the way through the long dry season.

Neither man said anything for the next couple of hours until Doc finally broke the silence. "You know," he said, "ever since we left town we've been riding through land that used to belong to one man."

Raider looked around him at the endless rolling acres of brushland. "Hell of a spread."

"His name was Lugo," Doc continued. "Jose Antonio Lugo, or Antonio Maria, I can't remember. Somebody told me his story once. He was the first white child born in Upper California. His parents were Catalan Spanish, like so many of the settlers here. Lugo started with nothing—

he was just a soldier and a peasant. But there was so much land here for the taking and so few people—the Spanish never numbered more than a few thousand in all of California, and the Indians had been made into simple mission slaves by the good padres, so men like Lugo could lay claim to all this real estate."

"Got real rich, huh?" Raider grunted. He wasn't paying a great deal of attention, but he felt somewhat relieved that Doc was finally sounding a little more like himself: windy.

"Well, not really," Doc said. "He had land and cattle but not much else. You know, Mexico let these people rot up here. Never sent them supplies, although they sure as hell taxed them. So when the Americans came back in forty-seven and eight, a lot of the locals, the Mexican governor included, wanted to throw their lot in with the United States. They'd have done that, right here in the little pueblo of Los Angeles, which is what it was then, but some thick-headed U.S. Marine officer in charge of a detachment of equally thick-headed Marines started abusing the locals. That offended the Angelenos' Latin pride, so they formed a group of lancers and had it out with the American troops. It wasn't much of an action—almost bloodless, I'm told, and very inconclusive—but the handwriting was already on the wall. There were just too many Americans coming into the area, and Mexico was in no shape to help, so we got the place."

"Not so good for the people who wanted to cozy up to the U.S., was it?" Raider replied. "Look at Lugo. He lost his land."

"Well . . . yes, but not in the way you think. I mentioned before that Lugo had lots of land and cattle but no money, and during the time the place was Spanish and Mexican that was all right. He could lord it over the Indian servants and put on a big show. He had that Latin love of display; he just *had* to show what a big man he was, with solid silver saddle blankets and all the most expensive imported gewgaws in his house, even if he didn't quite know what some of them were for. And to have all that he needed cash, so he borrowed. That worked out fine while the place was Latin. It was considered bad form to ask an important man to pay his debts. But when the Americans came, it was different—all business, no heart. The U.S. government ratified all those huge Spanish land grants, and men like Lugo continued to hold their land outright, but they couldn't stop borrowing to put on their fancy show, and, of course, when it came time to pay the money back, all they had to pay with was their land and cattle, and when the big drought came along a few years ago and wiped out so many of the cattle, that was the end of the Lugos, except, of course, for men like Pico, who had more to them than outward show. He kept his money and managed to fit into the new way of doing things. But as for the rest of the poor devils..."

"No, they don't look like they're doin' so good," Raider agreed.

Doc sighed. "I'm afraid the American race is not a very tolerant one."

He fell silent after that, and neither man said anything until they came to the small village of Santa Ana. For hours they had been riding through land planted in grapes and oranges. Raider picked a few oranges. "My God, a man could live off these things," he muttered, chewing inexpertly on an orange, the sweet juice running down his chin.

"Quite a land," Doc agreed. "A dry land, but give it a little water...."

Although they were tired and it was now full day, the two men decided to continue on. "We'd better make some miles," Raider said. "I got a feelin' those gamblin' friends o' yours are gonna be kinda persistent."

They were riding south through a broad valley, mostly uninhabited, and it was hot. The valley narrowed, which increased the heat. Both men were tired, sweat-stained, and dirty by the time they arrived at the old Mission San Juan Capistrano, with its small cluster of surrounding adobes. The mission was in a bad state of repair, but still the two men paused to admire the cool shaded garden within the old adobe walls. Then they pushed on.

"I can smell the sea," Doc said.

A few miles farther along, a wide pass brought them out onto the Pacific shore. They stopped their horses at the crest of a rise, wordlessly taking in the vast sweep of blue water.

"Let's find us a place," Raider said.

They camped beside a small stream that ran down a little draw only a couple of hundred yards from the surf. For once Doc didn't complain about sleeping rough. The continuous roar of the crashing waves soothed him. He lay for a while looking up at the stars, which were somewhat obscured by the sea air. Then he fell asleep. The same sound was in his ears when he awoke in the morning. They were on their way before the sun was fully up.

Inland, to their left, the land rose into rolling hills, mostly bare of cover except for brush and a few small oaks where there was a stream or a spring. By mid-morning they were passing along the western edge of the huge Santa Margarita Rancho, which had remained more or less intact. Just beyond was the small seaside village of Oceanside, where Raider marveled at the wideness and whiteness of the beach. By early afternoon they had passed Del Mar. A plateau lay ahead, with surf creaming against high, ocher-colored cliffs below. They rode up and over the plateau, across a mesa, and then down a winding canyon into the small town of La Jolla. A few small bungalows were spaced along a rocky, incredibly beautiful shore. Several miles farther along they detoured east around broad shallow mud flats. Hills ran down nearly to the water on the landward side. Then, crossing over the San Diego River, they entered San Diego.

Doc asked directions to the Horton House Hotel, which he had heard was one of the finest on the West Coast. The Horton House turned out to be an imposing pile sitting on a gentle slope overlooking San Diego harbor. The desk clerk looked askance at the two trail-worn men who appeared at his desk, but Doc's aristocratic manner soon had him hopping. Bellboys carried their meager store of belongings upstairs up to a pair of adjoining rooms.

Doc stood in the corridor for a moment, looking into his ornate quarters. "I like this, Raider," he said softly. "I like having money. I like living the way I was brought up to live."

Raider was less impressed. "Never did have enough money

all at one time to get the habit," he said dourly.

"That's just it, Raider!" Doc broke out fiercely. "Working for the agency, we're paid like paupers—*when* we're paid. Right now they're two months behind with our salaries."

"Guess that's the way it goes," Raider said, shrugging.

"Only if you let it," Doc muttered, then shut himself into his room.

Raider remained standing in the hall for a few minutes. Was that it? Was Doc worried about money? Not likely. He'd never paid much attention to money before. Yet for the past month . . . Ah-hah! Maybe that was it! Doc had been acting strangely ever since he'd tangled with that girl. The fancy one from back east, with the uppity airs. Doc had never said anything, but Raider sensed the girl had brushed him off, and done it none too gently. Ever since, Doc had been brooding, had been acting like some kind of animal was gnawing at his guts. He'd been neglecting his work, the agency, which had always been enough for Doc before. Yes, the timing was right. Well, damn, Raider thought, it was time to take some action. Dumping his gear in his room, he went down to the desk and asked the clerk where he could find the telegraph office.

Both men slept late the next morning. Then, once again washed and neatly dressed, Doc insisted on touring San Diego. They spent the late morning wandering the streets of New Town, or Horton's Addition, built by the same farsighted entrepreneur who had built their hotel. It was still a bit rough, but substantial buildings were going up. The sleepy Spanish pueblo was becoming a small city.

Doc ordered and ate a huge, lavish lunch at the hotel. Raider picked at his food; he was no gourmet. He watched his partner tuck away a pair of enormous lobster tails, along with several slices of abalone. "Doc," he said. "I got a question."

"Mrrmpphhh," Doc muttered around a mouthful of chewy abalone.

Raider hesitated. "Doc," he finally said, "were you really gonna gun down that gambler?"

Doc looked puzzled for a moment, then remembered the scene with thumbless Jake Bates in the card room. He swallowed the last of his abalone before replying thoughtfully, "I can't really say I have the answer to that, Raider. Perhaps I just wanted to make him sweat. I loathe his kind."

Then the desk clerk was signaling Raider from the entrance to the dining room. "Be right back," Raider told Doc. He returned a couple of minutes later with a slip of paper. "Got an answer from McParland," he said triumphantly. "He wants us in Denver as fast as we can make it."

"'An answer'?" Doc demanded.

"I wired him last night."

Doc looked coldly at his partner. "I'm not going," he said flatly.

"Awwww, Doc."

But Doc was not to be budged. He sulked in his room for a few hours, but late in the afternoon he knocked on Raider's door. "Let's go down to the old Spanish part of town," he said.

Glad to get out of doors, Raider followed. Old Town, as it was now called, was a longish walk to the north along the base of the hills ringing the bay, and Raider was not accustomed to walking. The old Spanish pueblo, a collection of adobes and a few wooden frame buildings, was situated on a flat portion of ground near the San Diego River. Compared to the bustle and newness of New Town, it was quite moribund, but Doc seemed to enjoy walking through its narrow streets and little plazas and peering into shaded patios.

His attention was caught by a largish adobe with a sign out front reading: RESTAURANTE. DELICIOSAS COMIDAS. Or rather, his eye was caught by the dark, smoldering beauty of the lovely Mexican girl busily wiping a table inside the open doorway. "I'm hungry, Raider," he said.

Raider was about to comment on Doc's seemingly endless appetite; he was only tagging along because he was looking for an opportunity to convince Doc to go with him to Denver. But then he too saw the girl. A slow grin spread over his face. "Yeah, I'm *damned* hungry."

The two men entered the house. It was clearly a private residence that had been converted into a restaurant. A low archway set into a thick inner wall led into a shaded interior. The girl looked up and did a quick appraisal of the two men. "Lupe!" she called.

"*Sí?*" A second girl came in through a side door, drying her hands on a towel. It was quite obvious she was a sister of the first girl. She too looked Doc and Raider over, her appraisal even more frank than her sister. "*Sí, señores?*" she asked.

Her voice was low and throaty, like her sister's. Both girls were dressed in long flowing skirts, showing an attractive amount of ankle and calf. White, low-cut blouses showed an even more alluring expanse of smooth olive bosom. Lupe was a little taller and more robustly built than the other girl, who was quite delicate. Both had thick black hair fashioned behind their heads in a long braid. Their dark liquid eyes held a fascinating blend of boldness mixed with a dash of alarm.

Doc informed the girls that he and Raider would like to eat.

"Maria, bring wine," Lupe ordered, giving one of the little tables an unnecessary wipe. As the girl bent over, Raider found himself staring down the girl's magnificent cleavage. He immediately fell in love. As he slowly sat down, his eyes lifted from that awe-inspiring vista and his gaze met Lupe's. Their eyes locked. Her breasts heaved. Raider started sweating.

Meanwhile, Docs eyes were following Maria's slender body as the girl undulated gracefully through a little doorway and disappeared from view. The clink of glass against glass suggested that she was doing as her sister had ordered, and indeed, a moment later she reappeared carrying two glasses and a bottle. Doc studied the way her breasts jiggled under the thin material of her blouse. Maria saw where he was looking and blushed. Now Doc was in love.

Doc unsteadily filled his and Raider's glasses with a dark red wine. His eyebrows rose in astonishment after he had tasted the wine. "Really quite good," he exclaimed. Flushing with pleasure, Maria pressed closer. Doc could smell the intoxicating odor of healthy young female flesh.

"Our family has been making wine in this very house for fifty years, señor," she said in a doe-soft voice.

The first bottle of wine went quickly, gulped down by feverish male throats as the two men watched the girls bustle about, preparing their meal. They both disappeared into the kitchen, and above the sounds of crockery and pots and pans, Doc and Raider could clearly hear excited giggling.

"Raider," Doc said quietly, "I think we have a chance."

"Gawd, Doc, I hope you're right," Raider said fervently. "Lupe..."

"A bit too much of the cow for me," Doc said with a gentle curl of his upper lip. "But now, Maria...that girl has the natural grace of a duchess."

The food came: beef stewed in a sauce of red chili; pork in green chili; freshly made tortillas, soft and hot; steaming tamales filled with spicy meat and a rich sauce. And, of course, more wine. As the third bottle thudded down onto the wooden tabletop, Doc looked up at Maria. "Would you and your sister join us in a glass of wine?" he asked.

Maria seemed to blush and hesitate. Lupe, however, ran to get two more glasses. There were now four at the table. Maria sipped slowly; Lupe took hearty swigs of the wine, her eyes sparkling more and more brightly.

"Sure am gettin' to like this kinda food," Raider said around a mouthful of tamale, while unsuccessfully trying to tear his eyes away from Lupe's breasts, so disturbingly near.

Lupe, Doc realized, was an easily attained objective. The girl was obviously waiting for Raider to make the appropriate move, her eyes excitedly running up and down his rugged body. Yes, a definitely obtainable woman. But what about her sister? Doc glanced quickly at Maria. She seemed to be growing more and more reserved. Or perhaps she merely had a different way of expressing her interest than her sister. Looking more closely, Doc noticed a deepening flush suffusing the girl's breast and climbing the slender column of her neck. She saw Doc looking at her and flushed even more deeply, and for the first time Doc had the impression—no, the certainty—that the flush had nothing to do with embarrassment or maidenly hesitation. The girl was wildly excited.

Acting on impulse, Doc simply slipped one hand inside the girl's blouse, and, cupping a marvelously warm breast in his palm, lightly pinched the nipple.

"Ooohhhhh," Maria gasped. Not a shocked oh nor an embarrassed oh, but a deep, thrilled, and—to Doc—thrilling sob of delight.

Raider's mouth dropped open as he witnessed his partner's bold move. He quickly looked over at Lupe. She looked back at him challengingly. "You do not like women?" she asked petulantly.

In reply, Raider sank both his big hands into the firm, abundant flesh of the girl's barely covered breasts. Her response was a soft sigh of contentment.

With all this mammary manipulation, the atmosphere in the room was becoming electric with tension, which Maria broke by abruptly getting to her feet and quickly walking to the front door, which she closed and locked. "Do you think we have enough time?" she asked her sister.

"I hope so," Lupe moaned, pressing Raider's hands more tightly against her breasts.

"Bueno. Vamanos." Maria urged Doc up from his chair. "Our bedroom is in the back," she said. "But we must hurry. You see, our brothers are out with the cattle, but they will be back soon."

By now both Doc and Raider would have followed the two girls into the middle of a pack of man-eating lions. The room they were taken to was small, with two beds, one against either wall, separated by a curtain. The beds were narrow and looked hard but were nevertheless very attractive to all concerned.

Raider disappeared around the other side of the curtain with Lupe, leaving Doc alone with Maria. "Oh, hurry . . . hurry," the girl said breathlessly as she quickly undressed. Doc was so enchanted by the slender, dusky loveliness of her naked body that for the moment he forgot to remove his own clothing. She stood naked before him, panting, her pert, firm breasts rising and falling quickly under the impetus of her excited breathing. "I love this . . . I love this," she murmured, taking Doc's hands and pressing them against her breasts.

He could feel how much her nipples had hardened, and then the girl was desperately guiding his right hand down her body. He felt his palm moving over the velvety smoothness of her belly, then into crisply curling hair, and finally, wetness, an amazing amount of wetness, his fingers driving into moist heat. He felt powerful inner muscles pulling at his fingers: The girl was having an orgasm already, still standing up. Then she was pulling him down onto the bed. He had no time to undress, merely time to lower his trousers, and then he was in her, his hardness driving deep into her gushing warmth. Her slender arms rose, closing around him, drawing him closer to her heaving, trembling, writhing body.

"Oohhhh," she moaned loudly, a wild cry of delight this time. "Ooohhhh . . . fuck me . . . fuck me"—her slight accent forming the key words, the ones which so excited Doc, into "Fock meee!"

And he did, marveling at how quickly this seemingly shy girl had turned into the whimpering, panting nymph writhing below him. From the other side of the curtain he was aware of giggles and low laughter, then a gasping cry from Lupe that indicated Raider was doing to her as Doc was doing to her sister.

It was short but intense, Doc finally spewing his orgasm into the girl while she had her fifth or sixth; he had long ago lost count. Raider's bull-like bellow from the other side of the curtain seemed to signal equal success. A short silence, then Lupe's throaty chuckle. *"Que hombre . . . que toro!"*

Doc looked down at Maria, still panting, her eyes huge and dark with surfeited passion, her breasts swollen larger now, her lovely skin damp and glowing. He felt himself growing excited again, but suddenly he heard the sound of hooves from outside the window, along with the jingling of spurs and a mutter of male voices speaking Spanish.

Maria stiffened under him. *"Madre de Dios!"* she hissed. *"Mis hermanos . . .* my brothers."

She was already wriggling out from underneath Doc. She stood in the center of the room like a frightened deer, naked, still flushed from their lovemaking, but quickly turning pale. "You must go!" she hissed.

Fortunately, all Doc had to do was pull up his pants, but when he dodged around to the other side of the curtain to give Raider the good news, his partner's jeans and boots were lying in a heap in the middle of the floor.

"Jesus!" Raider swore, grabbing for his trousers and nearly falling flat on his face as he tried to cram both legs in at once. Lupe remained lying on the bed, gloriously, voluptuously naked, looking speculatively up at Doc.

Yes, those really are some breasts, Doc thought. His eyes moved lower, taking in the wide hips, the deep swell of the stomach, the rich black triangle of wet matted hair punctuating the long lush sweep of naked thighs.

And then reality intervened. Someone was pounding on the front door. "Maria? Lupe? Why is the door locked?" a man shouted in Spanish.

"Mierda," another voice cut in. "They are at it again."

The pounding grew thunderous. "Quick . . . this way," Maria hissed, pointing toward the back of the house. Raider had one boot on and was hopping along on one leg while trying to pull the other boot into place. Doc was tugging his partner along, following Maria, who was still naked, her body shining softly in the deepening gloom. It was nearly dark outside.

Then they were at a back door, which opened onto a small garden. *"Vaya . . . vaya,"* Maria whispered urgently. Doc started out the door, then turned back and took the girl in his arms and kissed her on the mouth. She pressed herself to him fiercely, her nipples digging into his chest. *"Vaya con Dios,"* she murmured, and then shut both men out into the evening.

Raider had his other boot on now, and they both easily made it over the low adobe wall in back of the house. There was much shouting, screaming, and cursing coming from inside. *"Putas!* Whores!" a man was shouting.

"Pah!" Lupe shouted back. "You may speak like that the day you have a dowry to give us, but not before. We are not nuns...any more than you noisy little roosters are monks."

Leaving behind them this charming domestic scene, Raider and Doc quickly legged it down the narrow alley that lay on the other side of the adobe wall, heading for the lights of the main street.

"Yeah..." Raider was chuckling happily. "I sure as hell do love that Mexican food. Just the right amount o' spice."

Then he suddenly froze, motioning Doc back into the shadows. "What is it?" Doc demanded. "The brothers?"

"Uh-uh. A lot worse than that." And then Raider, keeping well back out of sight behind a bush, pointed out into the main street. There, only a dozen yards away, stood Gonzalez, the Bates brothers, and half-a-dozen heavily armed Mexicans.

CHAPTER FOUR

Discretion often being the better part of valor, especially against such one-sided odds, Doc and Raider tippy-toed their way out of Old Town, then made tracks back to the Horton House.

"It won't take 'em long to find out we're around," Raider muttered. "Not in a small place like San Diego."

"I imagine our recent lady-loves' brothers are spreading the glad tidings right now," Doc added.

So they were on the move again, quickly checking out of their hotel and securing their mounts. As they both swung up into the saddle, Doc said breezily, "Well . . . where to? The Mexican border's only fifteen or twenty miles south."

Raider glared at Doc. "I'm headin' for Denver."

"You're riding north? Right through our friends?"

"East. I'll pick up the train in Arizona."

Without another word, Raider turned his horse and headed away from the bay. Doc hesitated for a few seconds, then, with a good-natured shrug, rode after him.

They rode slowly at first; the moon wasn't up yet. Their

route took them upslope from the town onto a broad mesa.
Two hours later they rode down into a large valley, passing
the small village of El Cajon. Their route began to climb
as they headed up into the mountains, a formidable barrier
running north-south. About one in the morning they passed
Alpine, a small collection of cabins. They were in the trees
once again, and, finding a quiet grove near a stream, they
dismounted to catch some sleep.

"God damn! I'm gettin' tired o' this runnin'," Raider
groused as he laid out his bedroll. "I'm used to doin' the
chasin'."

"I'm rather enjoying the experience," Doc replied. "I
like the feeling of freedom it gives me, the sense of being
answerable to no one."

"Except to those gunslingers followin' us," Raider said
as he slid into his bedroll.

During the night Doc had second thoughts about the life
of a fugitive. He would have preferred spending more time
in San Diego, then perhaps going down a ways into Mexico.
He wanted to fill his days with activity, so that he could
forget.

Raider had hit close to the mark when he'd diagnosed
the cause of Doc's bizarre behavior. Somewhat more than
a month ago, Doc had been unfortunate enough to fall in
love with a beautiful, willful, and not particularly kind young
woman from a good Boston family. There had been passion,
there had been laughter, but when Doc had expressed the
seriousness of his feelings to the girl she had only laughed.
"But you can't be serious," she had said. "After all—"

"After all, what?" Doc replied around suddenly stiffening
jaw muscles.

"Why . . . the work you do," she had told him. "You have
no prospects, Mr. Weatherbee."

Doc had gotten up and left without a word, despite the
girl's halfhearted protests that he stay a while longer. He
walked the streets for hours, her words running through his
brain like corrosive acid. No prospects. The worst of it was
that she was right. He had no prospects—or, put more
simply, no money, no fortune, no commanding role in so-

ciety. And he knew that his particular proclivities, his endless wanderings, were unlikely to lead him to such a position.

Lying on the hard ground, watching the moon slowly
skim past the treetops, Doc let himself think about the girl.
It was the first time in weeks he'd let himself do that, and
as he thought, he realized that he was being a fool. But
common sense is seldom an adequate cure for unrequited
love. It was only a couple of hours before dawn when Doc
finally fell asleep.

The next morning's ride brought them to the booming
little mining town of Julian, near the top of a pass. The
mountains around them were quite heavily forested in pine
and fir. It was a lovely setting.

"Breakfast, Raider," Doc protested. "I've got to have
something decent to eat."

"Too damned late for breakfast," Raider growled.

"Then lunch."

They dismounted in the main street of the little town.
The saloons were already doing a roaring business. Peering
in through a set of swinging doors, Doc saw that a lunch
counter was already being set up. Early drinkers crowded
the bar, pouring down prodigious amounts of beer and whiskey—miners, most of them, and as hard-looking a group
as the work they did.

Doc and Raider entered and went through the formality
of ordering a beer before they headed for the piled-up food,
but to their surprise, there was no free lunch. "That'll be
four bits, fellas," one of the barmen informed them.

"Four bits!" Raider exclaimed. "That's highway robbery!"

"Then *you* haul the damned stuff up here."

So they paid their fifty cents apiece out of Doc's plentiful
supply of cash, loaded up their plates, and sat down at a
big trestle table, newly hacked out of fresh fir and smelling
agreeably outdoorsy. As he ate, Doc was automatically eyeing the others in the bar. They were throwing money around
with considerable abandon. Obviously the mines were producing well, and the sight of all that money began to appeal
to the new habit of acquisitiveness Doc had so recently

developed. Finishing his lunch, he stood up and moved to another table, one with a smooth, even top.

"Hey, where you goin'?" Raider asked.

Doc didn't answer. Reaching into his coat pockets he produced a large number of gold and silver coins and let them clatter noisily onto the tabletop. The sound of money seldom fails to attract attention, and a dozen heads swiveled in his direction. Stacking the coins neatly, Doc then took three shiny white objects from an inner pocket.

Raider saw what he was doing. "Oh, no, Doc, not the shell game," he hissed, but Doc already had the little half-spheres arranged in a line on the tabletop.

"Step right up, gentlemen," he called out in a quiet but clear voice, "if you're interested in a little game of chance."

The response was immediate. What miner, risking his life daily under miserable conditions, is not up to a game of chance? Mining itself is a game of chance. Several men drifted over, and Doc went into his spiel. He held up a small dark sphere, which he placed under one of the shells. Then, switching the shells around, he said, "All you have to do, gentlemen, is guess under which shell the elusive little ball is hiding."

"Hell, it's right under that there one," a tall, thin miner with a grizzled beard said loudly.

Doc picked up the indicated shell. Sure enough, the little ball was nestled beneath it. Doc looked chagrined. "You've got quite an eye, stranger," he said. "Would you like to put up money that you can do it again?"

"Ye'r damn tootin'," the man said eagerly, and slapped down a silver dollar.

Doc held up the little ball for all to see, and for all to see he placed it underneath one of the shells again. Then, moving his hands swiftly, he shifted the shells back and forth. "Which one?" he asked softly, looking up at the grizzled man, who was already eagerly pointing to one of the shells.

"Right there!" he bellowed.

And once again he was right. Eagerly scooping up one

of Doc's silver dollars, he was naturally eager to play again.
So were several others.

Sighing, Raider settled back in his chair and ordered
another beer. He watched as Doc artfully separated the
miners from a good deal of their money. He knew Doc
didn't cheat—hell, he didn't have to. He had incredibly
quick hands, as many a man who had tried to pull a weapon
on him had discovered. The ball was always there, and
always showed up underneath a shell, but not too often the
shell on which the majority had bet. Enough men won to
keep hope going in the others, but Doc's winnings were
steadily mounting. He was careful not to let too big a pile
of gold and silver accumulate in front of him. The surplus
disappeared back into his pockets in the most unobtrusive
manner.

The gamblers, however, were not totally unaware that
Doc was taking their money. In desperation, some of the
men were now playing with ten- and twenty-dollar gold
pieces in an attempt to recoup their losses. These were not
soft men, and Raider knew that if they got the idea they
were being fleeced, it was going to be right back up the
creek for Doc.

Raider slipped quietly out of the saloon. The horses were
still in front, tied to the hitching post, patiently waiting.
Raider checked them over to make certain they were in good
shape, then went around to the narrow alley in back of the
saloon. It was littered with trash. Poking through the debris,
Raider found some greasy old rags. Fastening one to the
end of a stick, he lit it with a match. It quickly caught fire
and began producing quantities of thick, evil-smelling smoke.
Raider held it up to one of the partially open windows at
the back of the saloon. The draft was in the right direction,
and the smoke slipped under the sill and poured into the
saloon's back room.

That oughta do it, Raider decided, and, dousing the rag
in a nearby rain barrel, he loudly shouted, "Fire!"

Raider was already sprinting around the side of the big
wooden building, heading for the front, by the time boots

were thudding toward the back room. He unhitched the horses and mounted his own only a moment before Doc came walking sedately out through the swinging doors. "Come on, let's get movin'," Raider said sharply.

Doc waddled to his horse, and, grunting, swung himself aboard. "This money is getting decidedly heavy," he complained.

They were around the corner and out of sight before anyone came out of the saloon. "You sure got a knack for makin' friends," Raider growled sourly. "If those hardcases from Los Angeles show up here, lookin' for us, we're sure gonna be remembered around these parts."

"What small portion of fame I'm able to attain, I am eternally grateful for," Doc said amiably.

They quickly rode up the slope leading to the east and out of town. After about twenty minutes, Raider pulled up his horse on a crest and looked back. Not only the town was visible below, but also a good deal of the slope leading down the other side of the mountain. Nobody was coming up their way from town; they must have been good losers. Then Raider suddenly stiffened in his saddle. Far down the mountain, a couple of miles short of the town, he saw movement. He stood in his stirrups, looking harder, and was able to separate the movement into several small moving black dots.

"Damn," he muttered. Swinging down out of his saddle, he reached into his bedroll and produced a pair of battered field glasses. They were powerful, and the distance was great, so he sat down behind a rock, steadied the glasses on the rock, and scanned for the distant figures. After a moment or two he picked them up.

"What is it?" Doc asked.

Raider took a long hard look before answering. "I ain't completely sure," he replied, "but I think it's those Bates idiots and that Mex, Gonzalez."

Doc's face darkened. "Damn," he swore softly. "I'm beginning to grow tired of their game."

"I got tired of it a long time ago," Raider muttered as he got up and replaced the field glasses. "Come on, let's get some distance between them and us."

It was a grim race now. They wove their way down a twisting mountain gorge. The air got hotter and drier the farther they descended. Rounding one bend, they saw far below them an enormous expanse of flat, sere desert. "I don't like the looks of that," Doc muttered under his breath. The hotter it got and the more tired he became, the less of his sense of humor remained. This was no longer a lark. It was no longer challenging. It was plain hard work.

They rode out onto the desert floor late in the day. The sun was low but it was still hot, with a strange desiccating wind soughing past, pulling the moisture from their tired bodies. They'd filled their water bottles at the last spring, but it was precious little for what lay ahead of them. Pointing their horses' heads east, and keeping the animals to a slow, energy- and water-conserving walk, they started across the desert.

"You remember Bill Miner?" Raider abruptly asked as their horses plodded along side by side.

"Certainly," Doc replied. "He's doing twenty to twenty-five years for robbing the Sonora stage, isn't he?"

"Sure is. You know, I met him once, a few years back after he got out of San Quentin. He did ten years there for the *first* time he stuck up the Sonora stage. He gets real talky when he's had a couple o' whiskeys, and he told me some real tales. You know, he rode over this same way, more or less, way back in '63. Seems the Apaches were on the warpath and some general needed a messenger. Bill was just a young squirt then, and built real light. He rode all the way across this desert in one night, delivered the message, then rode back the next night. Made some money after that, deliverin' letters for folks, but then he run outta money and started on the outlaw trail. That's when they nailed him for the first Sonora stage robbery."

"He always did have a thing for stages."

"Yeah. You know, everybody figures he was the man robbin' stages with Bill Leroy just before the vigilantes caught up with Leroy and hung him. Bill never said nothin' about that, but he did tell me he had himself a pile o' money saved up about that time, and used it to light out for London. You know—London, England? In Europe?"

"I've heard of the place," Doc said drily.

"Well, Bill said he had a good time there, till his money run out, then he got himself in with this Turk. Turns out the Turk was in the slave trade, stealin' Arab girls—you know, the ones that always got a handkerchief across their face—and he and the Turk'd sell 'em to harems. Bill had a lot to say about them harems."

"A sweet man," Doc said, partly to keep Raider talking. The desert made him nervous. It was so damned empty.

"Well, old Bill says he nearly got shot up by some o' them desert tribes, so he took off for South Africa. He was thinkin' o' robbin' a diamond train but said there were just too many guards, so he went down to South America and did some gun runnin'. You know how them people down there *always* got some kinda revolution goin'. That was just before he came back here."

"A genuine good-will ambassador."

"Did a lot o' robbin' for a while. He was one hell of a shot. One time he and his partner shot three possemen outta their saddles and made the rest give up the chase. . . . Hey. You smell smoke, Doc?"

Doc, who did not have the same natural trail senses that Raider had, did not smell it at first, but by the time they'd gone another half mile, he too smelled smoke.

"Don't smell like a campfire," Raider murmured.

Following the odor, they found the charred and still smoking remains of a small crude cabin a mile farther along. After carefully scouting the area, Raider led the way in.

"There's the owner," Raider said, pointing to a figure lying on the ground near the destroyed cabin. The moon was bright enough for them both to see, without dismounting, that the man had been scalped. Raider got down and poked around for a while. "Yumas," he finally said. "Wonder what put 'em on the warpath."

Suddenly the desert no longer seemed deserted to Doc. He looked around nervously, the wind-generated shadows behind every bush seemed to lurk with aboriginal menace.

"I think we should get the hell out of here," he said to Raider.

Raider nodded agreement and they remounted, continuing east. The moonlight showed them a line of sharp, stony ridges ahead, rising toward barren, lifeless mountains.

They made good time over the firm sand and reached the first of the ridges in a little more than an hour. It was from there, turning in his saddle to look back the way they had come, that Raider saw a faint gleam of light a couple of miles back. Out came the field glasses again.

"What is it?" Doc demanded. "The Indians?"

"Uh-uh. Gonzalez and company. I'll be damned if they ain't trackin' us by torchlight. That takes some real doin'."

Feeling even more hunted now, Doc and Raider rode higher into the rugged, rocky hills. They hadn't gotten far before Raider suddenly pulled his horse to a stop.

Doc nearly ran into him. "What now?" he asked.

"Sshhhhh . . . heard somethin'."

"Heard what?"

"Shut up!" Raider hissed angrily. "I think it might be Indians."

"Oh, God . . . our cup indeed runneth over," Doc muttered. "Gonzalez and the Bates brothers behind, a pack of bloodthirsty savages ahead. Why are you just sitting there, Raider? Let's get out of here."

But Raider continued to sit his horse quietly for a moment. "Come on," he finally said to Doc. "Maybe I got me an idea."

"But you're riding toward the Indians," Doc protested.

"Yep."

Doc had the choice of following or of being left behind. He followed. Raider detoured off the main route, moving in a big half-circle. Now Doc could hear the Indians too; they were surprisingly noisy. When he and Raider carefully edged around a big pinnacle of rock, he could see why. The Indians were drunk.

"Probably lifted some firewater off the man they killed," Raider whispered.

There were more than a dozen of the Indians, most staggering about drunkenly, some laughing and singing. Doc thought he caught sight of a scalp hanging from one warrior's belt, but he was too far away to be certain.

"You stay here," Raider whispered to Doc, then started moving his horse slowly down a little draw, heading straight toward the Indians.

"Wait...wait!" Doc hissed, but Raider was already a dozen yards away. Sweating with tension, Doc watched his partner ride closer and closer to the whooping, prancing braves. The brightness of their campfire, plus their inebriated condition, let Raider get very close. Doc saw him halt, a dark form behind a huge boulder. It was almost as if Raider were crouching to spring, then suddenly he put spurs to his horse and, with a wild whoop, rode right through the middle of the startled Indians, counting coup once, twice, three times, reaching down to touch individual men. And then he was gone, having done the most insulting thing possible—touching, unarmed, an enemy.

There was a moment of shocked silence in the Yuma camp, with only the sound of Raider's horse's hooves receding down the trail, and then with a wild scream of rage, the Indians leaped onto their horses, every man, and set off in pursuit of their humiliator.

Raider had a good start, but his horse was tired and the Indians began to gain on him. He used the spurs more than he was wont to, urging a little more speed from the animal. It wasn't much, but it was enough. By the time the Yumas had almost caught up to him, Raider had led them straight into Gonzalez and the Bates brothers.

The latter had, of course, seen the same burned cabin and scalped man as Doc and Raider, and now here were the Indians, whooping and shouting, sweeping down on them. Their reaction was automatic. Drawing their weapons, they opened fire.

Raider slipped into a small opening beside the trail at the last moment. The Indians, seeming to see their quarry melt into the mass of white men in front of them, and taking heavy fire, immediately found cover and returned the fire. A tremendous gunfight followed, the scalping party and the white men doing one another considerable damage.

Raider, ghosting quietly along the little draw, the sound of his passage lost in the tremendous din behind him, rode out of harm's way, chuckling softly. "There's some hombres that just rightly deserve one another," he murmured.

CHAPTER FIVE

They made it across the Colorado just after noon of the next day. There had been no more pursuit. Raider suspected that neither Gonzalez and Company nor the Indians had been in any condition to do more than lick their wounds and bury their dead.

The plan was to head for Yuma and catch the train east, then angle up into Colorado toward Denver. Both men were dog tired, and so were their horses, and the day was hot, so they drifted along slowly, neither man speaking. Doc, despite his fatigue, was feeling relaxed, as if the escape from Gonzalez and the Bates brothers had also freed him from a heavier, more hidden load. For the first time, he was looking forward to going to Denver.

They were riding slowly along a ridge top about thirty miles short of Yuma when they suddenly heard voices. "Someone's havin' an argument," Raider said.

"Out here?" Doc said, surprised.

The area was desolate and remote, not a sign of human habitation in sight. Raider motioned for Doc to keep silent, then quietly dismounted. Whoever was having the argument was hidden from view over the crest of the ridge. Doc, as curious as Raider, also dismounted and followed the bigger man. The horses, grateful for the chance to rest, remained obediently ground-hitched.

The voices were louder now. Doc heard something about a stagecoach. He joined Raider behind a large rock at the crest of the ridge and, hunkering down behind it, peered over.

There were two young men farther down the reverse slope, about twenty yards away, sprawled on the ground beside some boulders. "Dang it all, Harry," one of the men said to his companion. "I say we go ahead and do it."

"I don't know, Pete," the other man said. "We could git our asses shot off."

"Ah, shit!" Pete said disgustedly. "Never thought I'd hear a Jackson, an' my own brother at that, own up to a yella streak. If Pa was to hear—"

"Damn it, Pete," Harry shot back. "If Pa had any idea what we was thinkin' o' doin', he'd peel the hide right offa us."

Pete's voice was a little less certain now. "I hadn't figured on tellin' him," he muttered.

It was clear to both Doc and Raider that they were eavesdropping on an incipient stagecoach robbery. Pete and Harry both had rifles propped up against their boulder, aimed in the general direction of a rutted road below. The two would-be robbers appeared to be very young, probably no more than in their late teens. They were shabbily dressed. Doc wondered where their horses were, and then Raider was nudging him in the ribs.

"The rifles," he whispered.

Doc nodded, then carefully worked his way back to the horses, where he extracted both his own and Raider's Winchesters from their saddle scabbards. Retracing his steps, he rejoined Raider behind the big rock. Harry and Pete were still going at it heatedly. Raider took his rifle from Doc, then winked and eased the muzzle over the rim of the ridge. Doc did the same. Raider nodded, then both men worked the levers of their rifles, jacking a fresh shell into the firing chamber.

The harsh metallic sound, so awesomely full of meaning, was terribly loud in the midst of the surrounding desolation. Harry and Pete bleated dual whinnies of fright, twisting around to stare back up the slope.

"Move and you're dead," Raider snarled in his nastiest voice as Pete's hand strayed toward the butt of his rifle.

"I'm harmless . . . I'm harmless," Pete said shakily, skittering away from his rifle on his back, his hands jerking up over his head.

At first Harry seemed too petrified to move. He lay there, staring up at Raider and Doc, looming so huge against the skyline, then his hands shot up over his head. "Oh, God . . . don't shoot!" he pleaded.

Raider gave Doc a quick icy glance. "Whatta ya think?" he growled. "Should we plug 'em now, or take 'em back for the hangin'?"

"H-hangin'? W-w-what for?" Pete stammered.

His question was ignored. Instead, Doc said gravely to Raider, "I don't know. We're sworn to uphold the law, and now that we've finally caught up with the notorious Jackson brothers . . ."

"Be a lot easier to just shoot 'em," Raider said. "Never had much stomach for necktie parties."

"But we ain't *done* nothin' yet," Pete blurted. "Who . . . who are you, anyhow?"

"Pinkerton agents," Doc snapped, then added in his most impressive legalese, "And in the eyes of the law, intent is, in itself, a serious offense."

"A hangin' offense," Raider added grimly.

"Oh, God," Pete groaned. "How'd you know we was gonna do it?"

"The agency has its ways," Doc snapped cryptically. Pete looked up at him in awe. His brother lay completely unmoving, mouth agape, eyes terrified.

"Let's get it over with," Raider said, slowly raising his rifle. The Jackson brothers blanched and shrank even closer to the flinty ground.

"Wait!" Doc said. He pointed to Pete. "How old are you?" he demanded.

"Eigh-eigh-eighteen," Pete stammered.

Doc pointed to Harry. The boy's mouth worked silently for a moment. "S-s-seventeen," he finally managed to blurt.

"Mmmnnnnn..." Doc muttered thoughtfully, scratching his chin. "That puts a different light on things."

"Sure does," Raider grumbled. "We shoot kids, we got a lotta extra reports to fill out, and I hate reports. But if we take 'em in..."

"I see your point," Doc replied. He seemed to sink into deep thought. "Now, if I thought they'd never try anything like this again... Well! How about it? Will you?" he suddenly snapped at the two frightened young men.

Hope flared in two pairs of eyes. "N-n-no, sir," both boys exclaimed.

Raider chewed his lip for a moment. "All right," he said. "Get the hell out of here... back to your pa."

Pete and Harry slowly got to their feet, moving very, very carefully. They started backing down the slope, still staring up at Doc and Raider. Near the bottom, Harry slipped on some loose stones and rolled the rest of the way down, but he was on his feet in an instant and running down the road lickety-split ten yards ahead of his brother.

Both Doc and Raider continued standing on the skyline like grim avenging angels until the two young men were out of sight. Then Raider cracked. He'd been trying to keep a straight face, but now he choked and a loud guffaw forced itself past his lips. And then both men bent over, laughing helplessly.

"Oh, God, they're cured for life," Raider snorted when he could talk again.

"Every time they hear the word 'Pinkerton' they'll start looking over their shoulders," Doc agreed. "I think we nipped a crime wave in the bud."

The two detectives led their horses down onto the stage road and were in Yuma before dark. They rode straight to the livery stable and sold their horses. The next stop was the train depot, where, producing the railroad passes Pink-

erton agents were routinely supplied with, they checked their
saddles and other gear with the baggage man. A train was
due in two hours.

"A Pullman bunk is going to feel wonderful," Doc sighed.

"Let's wet our whistles a mite first," Raider suggested.
"That is," he added grimly, "if you can keep us outta trouble."

"I assure you, Raider, that trouble is the furthest thing
from my mind," Doc said fervently. He meant it. The scene
with the two would-be stagecoach robbers had been the final
catharsis, dissolving his pain into laughter.

However, trouble itself had other plans for the two detectives. Following the station agent's directions, they were
nearing the saloon when they noticed a small knot of men
standing in the street front. Both of them saw the long
sinuous shape of a bullwhip snake into view above the heads
of the crowd and flash through the air toward an unseen
target. They heard a meaty smack, then a laugh from the
watching men.

Raider and Doc moved up behind one of the watchers.
"Shit," Raider said disgustedly when he saw what was happening.

A tall, muscular Indian was swaying unsteadily on his
feet, facing a huge, barrel-shaped white man. The Indian's
hands were pinned behind him by two of the watching
crowd. The barrel-shaped man held the butt of a whip, the
lash laid out on the ground between himself and the Indian.
It was obvious that the Indian had already been struck several times; his buckskin jacket was cut to ribbons, and trick-
les of blood were running down his torso.

"What the hell's goin' on here?" Raider snapped to the
man he was standing behind.

The man turned and grinned, sending a wave of whiskey-
stink in Raider's direction. "Got us one o' them murderin'
Utes. Larry, there, is teachin' him how to act around white
men."

Larry was obviously the man with the bullwhip. He stood,
grinning through his thick black beard, aware of all the
admiring eyes. He was dressed like a mule skinner, a battered and dirty slouch hat hanging low over his eyes, his

drooping belt barely holding in an enormous belly. Raider
estimated the man's weight at about two hundred and
seventy-five pounds. His forearms were as thick as most
men's thighs.

"All right, you thievin', scalpin' savage," Larry roared
at the Indian. "Git down on yore knees in front o' civilized
folks, like I tole' ya, or I'm gonna crack ya one again."

The Indian stood rock still, impassive, his hooded eyes
meeting those of the bigger man. Not one line of his body
showed fear. This enraged the big drover. Snarling, he
flicked the shiny black length of the bullwhip out behind
him, ready to drive the tip forward again into the Indian's
bleeding body, but, stepping through the crowd, Raider
pulled his big bowie knife from its belt sheath and, with
one sweeping swing, cut the whip neatly in two.

Roaring with rage, Larry spun around, his little pig eyes
settling on Raider. Without a moment's hesitation he raised
the heavy, lead-loaded butt of the whip, ready to bring it
down on Raider's head. Raider messed up the man's timing
by quickly stepping in close and kicking his opponent in
the belly with the pointed toe of his boot. The big man
grunted, more startled than hurt. Raider's toe had sensed
the banded layers of muscle under all the fat, so he simply
continued forward and smashed the hard butt of his knife
handle against Larry's temple.

The big man went down like a stone, to the accompan-
iment of an angry roar from the crowd. Doc quickly slipped
into the center of the circle, his back to Raider's, while
Raider shifted his knife to his left hand and dropped his
right hand to the butt of his .44.

Seeing Doc standing apparently unarmed, a dirty, pock-
marked man with a week's growth of beard moved in front
of him. "No meddlin' strangers are gonna—" he started to
say, reaching for his holstered pistol.

Doc pinned the man's right hand to his side while his
Colt Lightning appeared in his own hand as if by magic.
He pressed the muzzle against the gunman's nose. "Don't
even breathe," he said in a soft but deadly voice.

This sudden show of force quickly cooled the ardor of

the rest of the crowd, most of whom were shiftless saloon hangers-on. A fair fight was not what they were looking for. The crowd began to break up.

Raider watched them go, then walked over to the Indian, who was now standing alone. "Your horse?" he asked.

The Indian, his eyes unchanging, jerked his chin in the direction of an Indian pony ground-hitched about forty yards away. Raider nodded in the direction of the horse. The Indian curtly nodded back, his eyes still showing nothing. Then, slowly and with incredible dignity despite his torn clothing and bleeding flesh, he walked over to his pony and vaulted aboard. Raider knew that must have hurt like hell, but the Indian's face remained expressionless. He sat astride the horse for a few seconds, motionless, looking straight at Raider. Then he nudged the horse, it spun around, and horse and rider galloped out of sight.

"I wonder what a Ute was doing way down here?" Doc said.

"Dunno," Raider replied. "Bad plannin', whatever it was."

Only four years before, after the bloody Adobe Wells fight, the Army had crushed the Ute Nation. A tribe that had once roamed over much of Colorado and the Southwest, the Utes were now restricted to a reservation in northern New Mexico and southeastern Colorado.

Doc and Raider took one last longing look at the saloon, but they realized their local popularity was at the moment pretty low. So they walked back to the train station to await their train.

About an hour later, after it had grown dark, Raider heard a muffled cry from beyond the waiting area. "Somethin's movin' over there," he hissed to Doc, ducking behind the station wall and pulling his partner with him. "Stay here and cover me."

Thirty-eight in hand, Doc watched Raider melt into the dark shade of some trees. He saw him again, or thought it was him, bending over something past the far end of the loading platform. A couple of minutes later Raider materialized out of the dark next to Doc.

"What was it?" Doc demanded.

"Our friend. The man with the whip."

"And . . . ?"

"Had a rifle. Probably gonna bushwhack us."

"You . . . stopped him?"

Raider shook his head. "Didn't need to. He'd already paid his dues."

"What the hell do you mean?" Doc snarled, exasperated.

"Somebody'd cut his throat," Raider replied. "And he'd been scalped. I kinda got a feelin' there's hair hangin' from a Ute belt right now."

CHAPTER SIX

Denver was a flat smoky sprawl ahead. The massive bulk of the Front Range, behind the city, looked like a painted backdrop as the train raced the last few miles across the plain.

"Gettin' bigger and bigger," Raider said dourly.

"A city of brick now," Doc added.

Raider's eyes tracked along the mountains to Long's Peak, all fourteen thousand feet of it. "I'll take the mountains anytime. It's clean up there . . . open."

"And cold and damned uncomfortable."

"Beautiful . . . free!" Raider insisted.

"How romantic. But you were born thirty years too late, Raider. The days of the mountain men are over. Forever."

"Yeah . . . yeah, sure, I know all that. But when I think of old Jed Smith . . . Grizzly Joe . . . Kit Carson . . . all this land, empty, game runnin' wild everywhere . . ."

"And the occasional Blackfoot or Crow scalping party," Doc added acidly.

"Ah, hell, that was just part of the fun," Raider replied with a big grin.

"Of course," Doc agreed wearily. It had been a long trip, across Arizona and New Mexico to circle the almost impassible barrier of the Rockies, which ran north-south through the middle of Colorado. Then by train, the Denver and Rio Grande line, to Denver. Days of travel, counting their journey—or rather, flight—from California.

"Wonder what McParland's got for us," Raider muttered.

The train rolled into the station. Doc and Raider took their few belongings and hailed a cab. Denver was indeed becoming a real city. The traffic on Larimer was hectic. At 16th the cab slewed sideways in the thick mud to avoid colliding with a heavy-goods wagon and almost upset.

"Goddamn!" Raider swore.

"Streets just need a little paving, that's all," Doc said. But he too was noting, after having passed through vast and open lands, the congestion and dirt of the city.

Their destination was the western headquarters of the Pinkerton National Detective Agency. The agency had grown enormously since Allan Pinkerton had founded it thirty years before. Now the old man was dead, and the agency was being run by his two sons, Robert and William—although it was William, working out of the original Chicago office, who was the most dominant of the two. However, they were both impressive men, big, physically fearless, and completely untiring in their pursuit of the lawless. Even Raider was in awe of Big William Pinkerton.

McParland, the Denver branch manager, was also a man of considerable repute. Many years before, he had made his name in the agency by infiltrating the Molly McGuires, an anarchist group suspected of many murders and a great deal of strong-arm activities in the mining camps.

McParland met them at the door. He was a big man, somewhat jowly now, wearing small round glasses and a large soup-strainer mustache that permitted only rare glimpses of his teeth. Doc noticed that he was a little more bald now, his thinning hair parted neatly a little to the left of center.

"You took your time getting here," McParland snorted by way of greeting, but the mud-stained, bedraggled state of his two star operatives softened his annoyance. "Well, come the hell in and take a load off your feet."

McParland remained standing as the two men seated themselves. He started to speak, then stopped, then started pacing back and forth, his hands clasped behind his back, big torso bent slightly forward, high forehead furrowed. "It's Tabor," he said. "It's got to be Tabor himself."

Doc's ears pricked up. "Tabor?" he asked. "The Silver Croesus?"

McParland nodded. "H.A.W. Tabor himself, the King of Leadville. You know about him?"

"I guess just about everyone does. He went from store-keeper to millionaire in just a few weeks . . . off the Leadville silver strike."

"Right," McParland said. "Staked a couple of sourdough miners to a few dollars in supplies and a jug of whiskey in return for a third share of whatever they found. And they found the Little Pittsburgh mine the next day. Tabor bought both his partners out and started buying up more mines— the Chrysolite, the Matchless. He takes in millions every year."

"So what's the problem?" Doc asked.

"Silver. A lot of it seems to be disappearing."

"High-grading? Or hijacking?"

"A little of both, although we suspect that most of it is being stolen from the mines themselves. There have been some robberies of silver on its way from the smelters to the Denver mint, but most of it never makes it to the smelters."

"Someone's stealing *ore?*" Doc asked in disbelief.

"We think so . . . if anyone's stealing it at all. That's the problem. How do you trace ore? The only thing we know is that production is down—way down—at Tabor's mines. Or at least the amount of metal coming out of the smelters is."

"Maybe his mines are just played out," Doc prompted.

"We thought of that. But the veins seem as rich as ever,

and there's a lot of activity down in those mines. Just not much coming out."

"And just in Tabor's mines?"

"As far as we know."

"But why only Tabor?"

"Well, uh..." McParland coughed uncomfortably. "There are some things you don't know about. Not too many people know about them—the whole story, that is. You see, Tabor is a big man in this state. Came up from nothing to be somebody. He's been lieutenant governor since '78. Gives a lot of money to the Republican Party and expects a lot back for it. He's...uh...got his eye on Washington now. Wants to be a U.S. senator from Colorado."

"Will money buy that?" Raider broke in.

"Well, it won't hurt," McParland replied. "You see, the Colorado legislature is going to elect a new senator in January for the regular six-year term. In addition, the President has recently appointed Colorado Senator Henry Teller as Secretary of the Interior, so the remainder of his term has to be filled. That's only for thirty days, though. Now, the Republican Party owes Tabor a lot, but a lot of people don't think they owe him a full six years in Washington. He's got some pretty powerful opponents for that post. About the only way Tabor can beat them is with money, and that's where the tie-in may be to this situation of disappearing silver."

"You think Tabor's political opponents may be trying to dry up his monetary power," Doc said.

"Perhaps...perhaps." McParland hesitated. "And then...there's another problem," he finally said. "A problem with a woman."

"Ain't there always," Raider put in.

McParland threw him a sharp look but met only bland innocence in Raider's black eyes. "Tabor's a married man," McParland continued. "His wife's name is Augusta, and a straighter-laced old girl would be harder to find. It seems she never quite got used to all that money. She's from New England, tighter than a tick, and keeps remembering the bad old days when they were scratching to make it. Now, Tabor's just the opposite. A more glad-handed, generous man you'll never meet. He's given away millions, and he wants to enjoy his money. His enjoyment tends to take the form of late nights playing cards with the boys, or playing other games with the girls. Augusta might have been able to take that. Tabor sent her off to Denver to live, built her a big Italian palazzo with hordes of servants so she didn't have to watch his goings-on in Leadville, but then, enter the spoiler. Baby Doe McCourt."

"Ah, I've heard of her. Supposed to be very beautiful," Doc said.

"Yes, beautiful," McParland said with sudden feeling, his eyes seeming to look far away. He shook his head. "And she's everything Augusta Tabor isn't—lively, cheerful, generous, ready for a fling anytime. The agency has done a little background work on her—Tabor wouldn't like that if he knew about it—and we found that she was born Elizabeth McCourt in Oskosh. She married a man named Doe whom she subsequently divorced. She came to Leadville in '80, when she was twenty-four, and immediately took up with a man named Jake Sands, born Sandelowsky, an old friend. Well, she eventually met Tabor, and he fell hard for her. Put her up in the best hotel in town—hell, *bought* one for her when he took her to Denver. And with Augusta living on her own in the big house, it was easy for them. But everybody knows, including Augusta. Our investigation shows that she's asking for separate maintenance. The whole thing's a huge scandal."

"With a scandal like that," opined Doc, "why bother stealing his silver to discredit him?"

"That's what I ask myself," McParland admitted. "Maybe this election thing and the decline in silver output are unrelated. Maybe somebody's stealing just for the money. *If* anything's being stolen at all. And those are some of the more important questions in this case."

"Who's asking the questions? Tabor?"

"Partially. And the government. Production is falling off at the mint because of the smaller amounts of silver coming in. The price is likely to rise, affecting the mint's operation. There are *lots* of people with questions."

"And we're the ones who are supposed to find the answers," Doc said.

"Yes."

"Undercover, of course."

"Of course. One of you in the mines, one of you working the angle of the election and the woman."

Raider placed his hand on the small of his back and groaned. "Guess I don't have to ask which one of us goes into the mines."

Doc smiled radiantly at his partner. "Brute labor becomes you so, Raider."

Raider smiled back at his partner, but it was a tight smile. "What do the Italians call those dudes who live off women?" he asked. "Jiggles? Jiggos?"

"Gigolos," Doc snapped, "And if you're suggesting . . ."

Raider sniggered. "It's all them pretty clothes you wear."

"Raider! You . . ."

"Gentlemen!" McParland cut in. "That'll be enough of that!"

McParland's innate authority was enough to quiet both Raider and Doc. The three men glared at one another for a few seconds.

"That's better," McParland said drily. "And now to work."

CHAPTER SEVEN

It had been an awe-inspiring train trip from Denver to Leadville, up into the Rockies. The scenery was stunning: huge peaks towering over deep-cut valleys, the foliage on the trees multicolored as the short intense Rocky Mountain autumn drew to a close.

The train didn't go quite all the way to Leadville. It was necessary to change to a stagecoach a few miles short. Doc, sitting alone, saw Raider, a number of seats ahead of him, pick up his traps and head for the exit when the train stopped at the switch-over point. Their eyes made brief contact, then slid away. Each had his own separate role to play.

Doc went back to the baggage car and made certain that his three large trunks were transferred to the stage. As the baggage handlers swung one down, it clinked slightly.

"What the hell you got in there?" one of the handlers asked. "Whiskey?"

"No. Medicine. I'm a homeopathic doctor."

"Too bad. I hear a barrel of rotgut whiskey in Leadville

can turn as much as fifteen hundred bucks profit."

"So can a few bottles of medicine, my friend," Doc replied equably.

Once he was certain his trunks were in place, Doc got into the coach. Raider rode on top. Traveling under a lesser social status, that of miner, his accommodations were necessarily a bit more Spartan.

The cover of homeopathic doctor was not new to Doc. Normally, when he used it, he traveled in a small Studebaker wagon drawn by a large and ornery mule named Judith. However, considering that Leadville was often snowed in for weeks at a time, Doc had not thought it a good idea to bring Judith and the wagon. The trunks would do.

The stage negotiated the last few rattling miles. Then, as it topped a small rise, Leadville came into view. Another typical mining boom town in Doc's eyes, for the most part consisting of jerry-built wooden shacks, muddy streets, and, capping all, a huge pall of smoke from the smelters. He did notice, however, as the stage descended toward the town, that there were quite a number of new brick and stone buildings. Obviously *some* people felt that Leadville had a future.

The streets were chaos: wagons, mules, burros, men on foot moving in and out of stores and saloons, and when Doc glanced into a back street, more men moving in and out of whorehouses.

Descending from the stage on Harrison Street, Doc quickly made arrangements to have his baggage taken to the Clarendon Hotel, which, he had been assured, was the best in town. It had been a source of amazement to Raider when McParland had made the reservation for Doc right there in the office, on that newfangled contraption, the telephone.

"What ain't they gonna think o' next?" Raider had murmured in awe. "You mean you can really hear 'em way over in Leadville?"

"I could if you'd shut up," McParland growled.

The telephone line from Leadville to Denver, McParland informed them, had been one of Tabor's many benefactions to Leadville. Another was the new opera house, the Tabor

Grand, a solid-looking brick structure a little farther down
the street from the Clarendon. Doc and Raider had each
been briefed as thoroughly as possible on their new client.
He, of course, did not actually know whom the agency was
sending. It was an agency rule that undercover operatives
be unknown to those who had requested their services, both
for the safety of the operatives and the effectiveness of their
operation.

"Tabor got to Leadville back around '77," McParland
said. "He set up a general store, along with Augusta, and
they did all right. Leadville was just starting to boom then.
There'd been a small gold strike back in the sixties, but it
petered out. Then somebody discovered that the slippery
blue mud that had made gold mining so difficult was in
reality almost pure carbonate of lead, with an extremely
high silver content. That's what made the boom, and Tabor
was in there early. Around '78 he got elected mayor and
postmaster, partly because he was one of the few available
for the job and partly because he was well liked. Not long
after that he struck it rich with the Little Pittsburgh. He
hasn't been stingy with his money. He's spent millions on
Leadville. He and some others started the fire department.
Rigged the men up in fancy uniforms with 'Tabor' written
big as hell across the front. And like most of the other big
silver barons, he's got his own private armies—the Tabor
Light Infantry and the Highland Guards. The Guards actually wear kilts and play bagpipes."

"What the hell's he need an army for?" Raider asked.

McParland shrugged. "For show, mostly. Tabor likes to
put on one of his fancy uniforms and parade at the head of
his men. Oh, there's some talk about having the men for
protection against Indians, but since the Utes got put down,
not much chance of trouble there. And for mine security,
of course. Hijackers."

"Doesn't seem to be doin' him much good now," Raider
drawled. "Maybe those private armies are kinda supposed
to keep the miners in line . . . in case they get uppity about
wages."

"Who knows?" McParland said uncomfortably, perhaps

because he himself had earned his spurs in the agency by fighting against labor. "But the thing is, Tabor's a big man in Leadville, and mostly a popular one. He shares his good luck. Loves to have himself a good time—women, cards, whiskey."

"I think I kinda like the man already," Raider said.

"A genuine philosopher king," Doc put in.

And that was the man they were working for, Doc thought as he walked along the narrow boardwalk toward the Clarendon Hotel, puffing a little from Leadville's ten-thousand-foot altitude. Beyond the town, Mount Massive thrust up into the background, dominating the scenery, reminding him Leadville was smack in the middle of some of the most rugged country in the world. The sun was out, but the air was thin and cold, and he shivered a little, remembering somewhat nostalgically the warmth of California.

The Clarendon was a pleasant surprise, a three-story structure of eighty rooms. The owner, Bill Bush, welcomed Doc himself. "Dr. Weatherbee," he said jovially, peering at Doc's signature in the register. "How long will you be with us, sir?"

"That's hard to say," Doc replied, somewhat bemused by a number of photographs which were prominently displayed on the wall behind the check-in desk. Quite an array of notables. Bush saw where he was looking. "All past clients," he beamed. "That's Oscar Wilde. That one's the Duke of Cumberland. That's General Sherman."

"Well, I see I'm in good company."

The room was comfortable, quite heavily furnished with an amazing array of bric-a-brac. Hot water was brought, and Doc quickly washed. Then he changed into his town clothes. Time to get to work. But first, of course, a bite to eat, and to Doc's amazement the food in the hotel's dining room was superb. "Wonderful," he enthused around a mouthful of pheasant. "How do you do it, way out here?"

Bush, who had been making the rounds of his dining room, beamed again. "Simple. I hired away the chef from Delmonico's in New York."

Genuinely refreshed, and hoping the job lasted—as long

as the agency was footing his bill—Doc went out into the
street. Night was coming on, and the streets were growing
increasingly crowded. The miners were coming up out of
the mines—single men, mostly, looking for food, drink,
and other fleshly attractions. Doc caught sight of Raider,
sitting glumly in the hiring office of the Matchless, one of
Tabor's richest mines. Their eyes met again, as on the train,
and once again, as on the train, slid past.

On Bill Bush's recommendation, Doc headed for the
Pioneer Club, one of Leadville's many watering spots. A
number of men were lined up at the beautifully polished
bar, downing their various brands of poison. Ladies were
noticeably absent, which did not please Doc, not simply
because he sought the company of women, but because his
assigned role in uncovering the mystery of Tabor's vanish-
ing millions lay in the direction of *cherchez la femme*.

Discreet inquiries led him in the direction of State Street,
Leadville's fun zone. Saloons were roaring wide open on
State Street, card games abounded, and so did the local
cribs. Once again acting on a tip, Doc entered a lush es-
tablishment at the better end of the street. The madam, a
somewhat portly but still very attractive woman of about
forty, dressed in a fortune in silk and velvet, sauntered into
the parlor to inquire as to what the gentleman's particular
tastes might run to.

Doc introduced himself as he looked around at the half-
dozen lovely and well-dressed young women sitting or moving about the parlor. Most were as yet unmarked by the
stresses of their particular way of earning a living. "Someone
suggested I ask for Kitty," he ventured.

It had been McParland. "She's had a thing going with
Tabor," the chief detective had said.

The madam gave a little bow. "That someone has good
taste." She gave a signal and one of the girls got up and
left the room. A drink was brought for Doc while he waited,
and by the time he'd half finished it, the messenger returned
with another girl. She stood looking about her for a moment,
a tall, lushly built young woman. When she saw Doc a
smile lit up her face. A whore's smile? Doc wondered. No,

there was more to it than that. Too spontaneous, too un-
forcedly cheerful. This girl likes to smile. She likes life,
Doc thought. And I think she likes me.

"You asked for me?" she asked in a voice just as cheerful
as her smile. She has a good face, Doc decided. Open,
positive, ready for anything.

Doc allowed as how he had indeed asked for her. "Who
told you about me?" she asked.

"A friend in Denver."

"No name?"

"He would rather I didn't use it."

Doc didn't really have to say that, but he was interested
in the girl's reaction. A look of annoyance crossed her face.
"Another lily-white pillar of the community, no doubt," she
snapped. "Happy enough to...But never mind." And that
fresh smile was on her face again. "I hear your name's Doc.
We'll pretend we just met in a tearoom. Want to go someplace a little more private?"

"I would be delighted."

"Okay, come on, then." The girl turned, hitched up her
full skirts, and started up the same stairway she'd just descended. She bounded up it with remarkable verve, leaving
Doc to chug along behind, admiring the way her hips sway
and jiggled ahead of him. Damn this altitude, he thought.
Hard to breathe.

She took him to a large room, furnished not only with
the most obvious tool of her trade, an enormous bed, but
also with a rather nice suite of furniture. Kitty perched
jauntily on the edge of the bed and waved Doc to a chair.
"I like you," she said.

"Oh, really?"

"Yes. You smell good. Some of the men who come in
here..."

Then, as if realizing that reminding Doc of the legions
who used her body was probably not the most intelligent
ploy, she simply said again, "You smell good."

"How can you tell...way over there?"

"Well, if I *could* smell you from way over there, like
some of the others..."

Realizing she'd done it again, Kitty suddenly blushed, which instantly captivated Doc's heart. A damn nice kid, he thought. Probably no more than twenty, and so damned full of life. He wondered how long it would take for her present way of life to squeeze out that freshness. Never, he hoped. But in a mining town of thirty thousand, with the majority of the population men . . .

"Would you like me to take off my clothes?" Kitty asked with disarming frankness.

"Why . . . yes, I think I would like that," Doc replied. "Do you mind if I just sit here for now and watch?"

"Of course not," Kitty said as she began to work with buttons. Then she stopped, a hesitant look on her face. "Say, you aren't one of those strange kind, are you?"

Doc laughed. "No, as I hope to prove to you a little later. It's just that you are so lovely and . . . fresh. I would like to think that I am waiting for you to emerge from all that cloth like watching a butterfly emerge from its cocoon."

Her face lit up. "What a pretty thing to say."

She continued undressing, taking obvious delight in Doc's equally obvious appreciation of her body as layer after layer of clothing was peeled away. Naked to the waist, she placed her hands under her bare breasts and lifted them a little. They didn't lift far; they appeared to be solid as hell and were pleasingly large, without being grotesquely so. "Everybody says I have nice tits," Kitty said bluntly.

"Everybody's right," Doc murmured, admiring the two big mounds. Kitty absently flicked her nipples. They instantly began to pucker. "*I* like my tits too," she said.

A lot of bloomers and petticoats remained to be peeled away. "I wear all this stuff," she confessed, "because Claudia—that's the woman who owns the place—says it gets some men excited. . . . Oh, darn, there I go again, saying the wrong thing."

Doc laughed. "Don't try to change yourself for me, Kitty. I like you just the way you are."

She grinned impishly. "Really? Does that mean you don't want me to take off the rest of my clothes?"

She had been pushing the last pair of bloomers down

over her lush hips. Doc could see the top edge of pubic hair, a lovely burst of brown.

"I think you can guess the answer to that," he murmured.

She smiled, teasing him by first starting to pull down her bloomers, then pulling them up again. Then, suddenly, she slipped them down over her thighs and, bending forward, worked them free of her legs. When she stood up straight again, she was totally naked, and as lovely a young woman as Doc had ever seen, lush, glowing with health and energy, her large taut breasts jiggling a little as she tried to suppress a giggle. A perfect V of brown fur nestled high up between her soft thighs.

This is nice work when you can get it, Doc thought, feeling a stirring in his loins as he looked at the naked girl. He stood up and started toward her.

"Say, mister," she said with a giggle. "Is that a gun you're hiding in the front of your pants?"

Doc looked down and saw that an erection was tenting out the front of his trousers. "Suppose we just find out," he murmured.

"Oooohhhhh . . . are you going to stick me up with it?" Kitty squealed in mock fright. "Or maybe you're gonna stick me in."

Her voice was a little more husky now as Doc walked toward her. He reached out and slowly caressed her breasts. He liked the solid weight and the velvety feel of them, liked the hot rubbery pucker of her nipples.

She gave a shaky little laugh. "You've found one of my weak spots," she sighed.

"You have others, I suppose," he murmured. Her fingers were tugging at his shirt buttons. Amazing how cleverly and quickly she got him out of his clothes. Her fingers closed around the shaft of his achingly hard cock. "No, you're not one of those strange fellas," she said huskily. "Oh, for God's sake, Doc . . . put that damned thing inside me!"

My God, she sounded genuinely excited. He looked closely into her face, to see if she was merely pulling whore tricks, and he decided she wasn't. A whore who genuinely likes to fuck, he thought. She'll never last in this trade.

He pushed her down onto the bed. His hand slipped up between her thighs, found softness, heat, wetness. "My other weak spot," Kitty panted. "Oh, please forget about your fingers. Put your cock in me."

Doc fell on the girl. Her legs opened eagerly. A moment's probing and then he felt himself being swallowed in moist heat. Kitty's body surged upward, met his.

"Deeper!" she panted. "Deeper!"

Doc did his best as her body flexed beneath his, her flesh firm and warm, her muscles working smoothly, her breasts hot and firm against his chest. Her legs rose, wrapping around him, and he drove into her hard.

"Oh, yes!" she gasped, laughing delightedly. "That's the way I like it!"

She either came several times over the next fifteen minutes or she was one of the best actresses Doc had ever met. Her healthy vibrant young body drew vast reserves of energy from Doc, despite the high thin air of Leadville. Panting, he continued making love to the girl, watching her mouth open in astonishment each time a new orgasm rippled through her body. Finally, he could not hold his own back.

"Oh . . . it's so hot! So damned hot!" she squealed as he came inside her.

She was like a playful kitten after that, rubbing her body against his as he lay exhausted on the bed. "Did you like that?" she giggled, but Doc couldn't answer directly because she had shoved a large portion of one of her breasts into his mouth, so he nodded instead, the resulting motion making the girl's eyes go all dreamy again. Doc was tempted to renew the game, but business called.

"Kitty," he said, pulling loose from mammary temptation, "what are your plans for the rest of the evening?"

The absurdity of his question did not strike Doc until he saw the look of amazement on the girl's face. They both burst out laughing at once. "Let me put it another way," Doc amended. "What would it take to have your company for the rest of the evening?"

"Money," the girl said simply. Doc looked more closely

into her face, noticing now that slight trace of hardness, the mark of the professional. Kitty was aware of his appraisal. "You haven't asked me yet," she said in a rather chilly voice, "what a nice girl like me is doing in a place like this."

"Getting rich, I hope," Doc shot back. "And if the last half hour is any indication, doing what you most like doing."

She looked long and hard at Doc to see if he was making fun of her—and decided he wasn't. "Oh, I'm getting rich all right. I'm trying like hell to save my money. But as for doing what I like best, it's not always that way, not by a damned sight. Some of the men I have to . . . well, they're not all like you, Doc."

A clever choice of words by a whore? No, he didn't think so. He patted the girl's round, slightly damp ass. "Come on," he said. "Let's get dressed."

Kitty looked disappointed. "You've changed your mind about tonight?"

"Uh-uh. I just don't want to spend it all here. I want you to be my guide tonight. Show me Leadville."

The girl smiled. "I'd like that, Doc. I'd like to be seen with you. We'll do it. That is . . ."

"What?"

"As long as we end up back here," she said, patting the bed and favoring Doc with a slow sexy smile.

CHAPTER EIGHT

For a whore, Kitty was the slowest dresser Doc had ever seen. However, the results justified the wait. When he and Kitty finally sallied forth from Madam Claudia's House of Joy, Doc had a genuine butterfly on his arm. Kitty was dressed to the nines, wearing a long wine-colored gown, a fox-fur wrap, and a glorious hat crowned with ostrich plumes. Radiating her usual vitality, the girl swung along jauntily beside him as they stepped out onto Leadville's notorious State Street.

The street was going full blast, thronged by crowds of people: roughly dressed miners, smelters, riggers, drovers, teamsters; an occasional hunter from the mountains in trail garb; slickly dressed gamblers; stolid businessmen out for a night of therapeutic sin; the entire kaleidoscopic spectrum of a booming mining town.

"Look—there goes the competition," Kitty laughed, pointing to a gaily decorated barouche drawn by a pair of matched bays, working its way slowly through the crowds. An enormously fat sporting-house madam, no mistaking her calling, sat arrogantly on the seat, the reins clutched between fat, be-ringed fingers, a huge meerschaum pipe clenched between massive jaws.

Doc marveled at the woman's high-piled mass of bright orange-dyed hair. "Now *that's* class," he said.

Kitty laughed gaily, walking like a queen past the grimy little one-girl establishments that spread up and down the street. That was the end of the line for a fallen woman—alone, ruined, no one to protect them from their more brutal customers. Doc had a momentary image of Kitty, in ten or fifteen years, if she continued in her present line of work, jaded, without hope, finishing her life under similar circumstances. He hoped not.

They passed the Bucket of Blood saloon, aptly named, then on past fortune-tellers' stalls and peep shows. A little farther down the street Doc noticed two blazing bonfires suspended in big iron tubs above a sprawling structure. "What's that?" he asked Kitty.

"Mabel Rivers' Athenaeum. You want to go in?"

Doc nodded and Kitty led the way into a large amphitheater. On the stage below, two huge, half-naked women wrestlers were grunting and straining. An animal act waited in the wings. Doc and Kitty took seats, Kitty enthralled by the performance, Doc idly scanning the crowd. It was an incredibly heterogeneous collection of people, lacking only in well-bred ladies with a reputation to maintain; but in general, women seemed plentiful.

Doc's eyes were drawn to one particularly lovely specimen, a woman in her early or middle twenties. An abundance of soft flesh was doing its best to escape from her well-cut gown, but she was not fat. Ripe was the word that came to Doc's mind. Her carefully curled hair was piled atop her head, framing a lovely oval face and highlighting large soft eyes. The picture was one of such artless sensuality that Doc, lost in his admiration of the woman, did not at first pay much attention to her male companion. He was a big man with a high forehead, piercing dark eyes, and one of the largest handlebar mustaches Doc had ever seen. Only slowly, remembering the photographs he had seen in McParland's office, did Doc realize who he was looking at. "Isn't that H.A.W. Tabor?" he asked Kitty.

She followed his gaze, looked at the man for a few seconds without moving, then said, "That's him, all right."

"And the woman?"

"Baby Doe," she replied flatly.

"I gather she's not one of your favorite people."

"Oh, I haven't really got anything against her. It's just that Tabor, well...he used to be kinda sweet on me, an' then Baby Doe came along and, well..."

"She stole him away?"

"Oh, hell, it wasn't like that. I'm just kind of acting silly. Old Horace was sweet on a lot of us girls. Hell, he brought Willie DeVille out here from Chicago. She was working in one of the best houses there, and he had that girl that used to run the wild animal act...but never mind all that. It was all over when he met Baby Doe."

"Love at first sight?"

"Well, they sure wanted to get in each other's drawers, but maybe for different reasons. Hell, I shouldn't say that. I think Baby Doe's just out for a good time...like me. Course, it don't hurt if that good time comes along in the shape of six feet of millionaire. My God, *look* at those diamonds he's bought her!"

Baby Doe did indeed sparkle, from the emeralds in her hair to the magnificent diamonds suspended from her neck and dipping tantalizingly into one of the more memorable cleavages Doc had seen in a life devoted to the admiration of cleavages. She was a damned fine-looking woman, no doubt about that, and his immediate reaction was to admire her, although he had to remain aware of the possibility that it might be she, Baby Doe, worming her way deep into Tabor's confidence, who was plundering him.

"How did they meet?" he asked Kitty. "Did he send for her too?"

"Uh-uh. She's a divorcée, you know," Kitty said haughtily, showing Doc a glimpse of unsuspected snobbery. "She came here from Central City back in '80. She had a friend here, Jake Sands, and for the first few weeks she was here they really hit it off. Jake put her in a boardinghouse, and you can believe me, neither one of 'em had too many lonely nights. I got a feeling Baby Doe really loves it. Fucking, that is," she added bluntly.

"Like you?"

Kitty gave him a flaming smile. "You bet your ass, mister," she chuckled.

"I'm more interested in yours."

"You'll get another chance at it later," she promised. "Anyhow, I guess Baby Doe started noticing Tabor; you can't hardly miss him in Leadville. Hell, he runs the place, always out parading in front of one of those comic opera armies of his, or just sporting around town, once he sent his wife off to live in Denver. Anyhow, Jake used to like to go play cards in Pap Wyman's place, and he was up there one night, losing more than he knew, because Baby Doe, on her own for once, went down to the Saddle Rock Café, and lo and behold, who does she run across but old 'Haw' Tabor himself. The way I hear it, Tabor nearly fell out of his chair when he saw her, and that was that. A few days later he had her set up in a fancy hotel as his personal property. Scratch Jake. Baby Doe gave Jake a big diamond ring, though—I guess she got it from Tabor—to make it up to Jake. Jake's a hell of a nice guy. And one thing you gotta say about Tabor and about Baby Doe, too—they're not tightwads. A couple of the most generous people I've ever met."

"You . . . liked Tabor, then," Doc asked casually.

"You mean, could he get it up?" Kitty hooted. "Hell, yes. He's kinda crude, not a gentleman like you, but I don't think there's a mean bone in his body. Not *real* mean, anyhow."

A troupe of tumblers was on the stage at the moment, and the next billed attraction was "Woman Bathers," which was mildly interesting to Doc but not terribly so. Particularly not when he noticed Tabor, with the lovely Baby Doe on his arm, making his way toward the exit. It was more like a progress, with Tabor greeting and being greeted by almost everyone he passed. He was obviously a very popular man.

Doc waited until they were out of sight, then said to Kitty, "Would you mind terribly if we left?"

"Uh-uh. Let's go get us some champagne," Kitty said eagerly. "I sure as hell love that stuff."

More than the head office is going to love my expense account, Doc thought. But what the hell. If they wanted results, they were going to have to pay for them.

As he had hoped, by the time he and Kitty made it out into State Street, Tabor and Baby Doe were still in sight, still greeting well-wishers. Doc watched Tabor hand Baby Doe into a magnificent carriage, but instead of climbing in after her, Tabor shut the door, then kissed her through the open window.

"Well, you don't see too much of that . . . him letting her go off alone," Kitty said. "Sometimes I think he's afraid she'll just vanish like a puff of smoke if he lets her out of his sight. Only one thing I know of that can get him to do that. He must be going up to Pap Wyman's."

"The gambling place you told me about?"

"That's the place. Hell, the amount of money Tabor loses in there could set me up for life."

"Do they serve champagne?"

"Of course. It's a high-class place."

"A little gambling would be pleasant. They do let women in, don't they?"

Kitty laughed. "Sure . . . my kind of woman."

Kitty was looking after Baby Doe's disappearing coach with a certain degree of wistfulness. As a divorced woman, Baby Doe had a social position only slightly up the pecking order from Kitty's but not much—just below that of actress. Divorced women were considered, in the better orders of society, to be a walking scandal. But still Baby Doe retained enough status to be a cut above going to a private gambling hall like Pap Wyman's. Kitty, however, was beyond the pale, a thought which saddened Doc. He liked the girl.

Oh, stop being a snob, he warned himself.

CHAPTER NINE

Pap Wyman's place was in keeping with the many other pleasant surprises Doc had so far experienced in Leadville. Behind the rather unprepossessing exterior of a large false-fronted structure, the gaming rooms inside were quite plush. It was all there: poker, twenty-one, roulette, craps, with the action going strong. Kitty turned heads when she entered, which also drew attention to Doc, about which he had mixed emotions. However, not even Kitty's loveliness was enough to draw the players' attention away from their play for more than a few seconds.

Tabor was already seated at one of the poker tables when Doc and Kitty came in. He too looked up at Kitty, but he added a smile and a wave. Kitty sent back her own halfhearted, wistful little wave.

Doc steered the girl over to the blackjack table, where he took a seat. Kitty stood just behind him, her right hand lying affectionately on his shoulder. A waiter came bustling up and took Doc's order for both drinks and chips. The champagne, genuine French bottling, was served to them in a silver ice bucket with lovely beads of condensation frosting the outside. The glasses were crystal.

Kitty seemed quite contented, squealing excitedly each time Doc won a hand, which was more often than he lost. Doc was not interested in games of pure chance, such as roulette. He preferred poker or blackjack, where skill and patience usually brought him out ahead of the game, far enough ahead tonight, he hoped, to pay for some of the champagne Kitty was so enthusiastically pouring down her lovely throat. No point in letting the expense account get *too* far out of hand.

From where he was sitting, Doc had a clear view of Tabor. He was obviously a bit in his cups, but not playing too badly, as the healthy stack of chips in front of him testified. He was laughing, joking, telling dirty stories, and, all in all, appeared to be having a fine time.

Kitty had been bending forward periodically, whispering little endearments and bits of social information into Doc's ear, and in the process distracting his play somewhat because of the insistent pressure of one of her breasts against the back of his right arm. Suddenly she bent down and hissed, "Uh-oh, here comes trouble."

Using his peripheral vision, Doc was aware of someone just entering the room and approaching Tabor's table. Doc completed the play of his hand, and, while the dealer was scooping up the cards, he casually glanced to the side. A tall hard-faced man, dressed in dark well-cut clothes, was standing quite still, looking intently ahead. The expression on his face was not easy to decipher except for one element—hostility, and Tabor seemed to be the target of that hostility.

Kitty was bending forward again. "That's Jack Harrison," she whispered. "Hates Tabor's guts. I hope there isn't going to be any trouble."

Tabor now seemed to become aware of the newcomer. He looked up, his eyes blinking once as they met Harrison's stare, then Tabor's eyes steadied and he smiled lazily. "Howdy, Jack," he said. "What brings you out this time o' the night? Gonna go out and do a little midnight claim-stakin'?"

"You haven't left the rest of us much for the claiming, Tabor," Harrison replied in a controlled but rather menacing voice.

Tabor didn't reply directly. Instead he said, "I'd invite you to set a spell and play a few hands with us, but as you can see, all the places are taken."

Harrison nodded. "Seems I've heard more or less the same thing from you before," he grated. "Fortunately, I really don't find the offer all that attractive."

He turned away and went over to the roulette table, where he began playing with a furious recklessness. Kitty's breasts pressed against Doc's arm again, and her warm sweet breath tickled his ear. "They hate each other," she murmured. "Well," she amended, "as much as Tabor can hate anybody."

"That's clear," Doc said. "But why?"

Kitty shrugged. "I think originally they just kinda rubbed each other the wrong way, but it really came to a head when Tabor accused Jack of claim-jumping. It was probably true, but Jack doesn't like to have that kinda thing said about him, so he struck back by having some of his crew bust up a few of Tabor's men. Tabor almost called out his Highland Guard over that, but Jack backed down just in time to head off a full-scale war."

"What do you mean, Harrison's crew?"

"Part of his smelter crew. Jack used to have one of the biggest smelter and crushing mill outfits in Leadville, and that's how Tabor got back at him. Wouldn't send him any more of his ore, and got some of the other big mill owners to follow suit. Jack's mill ain't so big anymore. Sometimes I wonder how he keeps it open."

"He doesn't seem to be hurting much for money," Doc observed, watching the way Harrison seemed to be throwing it away at the roulette table.

"Well, there's so damned much of the stuff in this town, Doc."

Apparently so. Doc glanced over at Tabor, the custodian of so much of that money. The big man was continuing to play poker as if nothing had happened, cheerful, smiling, joking. But Doc noticed that from time to time he would covertly glance in Harrison's direction, and it was not a friendly glance.

Doc continued to play for a while longer, which included a second bottle of champagne. Kitty was growing quite tipsy. "Come on, Doc," she whispered into his ear. "Let's go back to my place. We got champagne there, too."

And a lot more than champagne, Doc thought, intensely aware of the fullness of Kitty's body behind him, aware too of her growing amorousness. When he looked up again he noticed that Jack Harrison was no longer playing roulette. In fact, he was no longer in the room. I've been paying too much attention to pussy, he chided himself. Tabor was still playing poker, however. Oh, what the hell, Doc thought. It's my first night in town, I've already learned a great many things, I'm tired, and of course, there's the girl.

"All right," he said, turning around, his cheek grazing Kitty's bosom. "That's a great idea. Let's go back to your place."

He cashed in, eighty dollars ahead. Not a fortune, but it might pay for the night's champagne, considering the way Kitty seemed capable of putting the stuff down. Champagne seemed to excite the girl. He could feel her body trembling as she took his arm. Her face was flushed, her eyes shining as she looked up at him.

"Oh, Doc," she chuckled. "When we get back, I'm gonna teach you some things."

Doc smiled, thinking, There's not much you're going to teach me, my lovely young friend. In fact . . .

As they stepped out into the street, Doc was so preoccupied with the girl that he didn't notice the activity in an alley entrance a few yards away until he heard voices. Glancing quickly in that direction he noticed several dark shapes well back in the alley and instinctively took evasive action. It paid to be careful in a place like Leadville.

The men in the alley had apparently not seen Doc and

Kitty. Doc stepped out of what light there was. He heard some more muttered words from the alley, then a man saying in a rough, coarse voice, "Okay, Jack, another run tonight, then."

At that moment someone lit a lamp in the building next to the alley and the light spilled out through a window into the night, illuminating the little group standing in the alley. To Doc's surprise he recognized one of the men as Jack Harrison. He was facing a big, heavily built man in working clothes. They both blinked and shied away from the light, then Harrison said hurriedly, "Right. I'll be expecting it," and then turned and headed back for the mouth of the alley and the street.

Doc, not wanting to look as if he'd been spying, began walking along again, his arm around Kitty's shoulder, nuzzling her neck as if they'd been kissing in the shadows. Harrison saw them the moment he stepped out onto the narrow boardwalk and did a quick double-take, staring intently at Doc and apparently recognizing him from Pap Wyman's. Harrison started to walk away down the boardwalk, paying so much attention to Doc that he failed to notice two miners wobbling out of a saloon doorway just ahead of him, obviously the worse for drink. Harrison ran straight into them, ricocheting off one of them and nearly losing his balance. "Look where the hell you're going, you ignorant hayseeds," he snarled, trying to push on past.

But one of the miners grabbed his arm. "Hold on there, big-mouth," he slurred drunkenly. "Was you who run inta us, so don't be given' us none o' your lip."

Something seemed to snap inside Harrison. The miner, a good-sized man, was just pulling back his fist when Harrison kicked him in the kneecap. The man bellowed in pain and bent forward just in time to catch Harrison's fist straight in the face. He staggered back, out of it for the moment, while Harrison turned to his companion, who had been watching the entire proceedings goggle-eyed. Harrison kicked him in the belly, then chopped him down the way a person might chop down a patch of weeds, hacking with his fist, driving the man toward the ground.

Meanwhile, the first miner was trying to get to his feet, blood streaming from his mouth. Harrison spun around and kneed him in the face while he was still only halfway up. Although he was several yards away, Doc could clearly hear the man's nose crunch. He himself might have stayed out of it if Harrison had not begun kicking the man as he lay moaning on the ground.

Doc quickly stepped forward and took hold of Harrison's upraised forearm. "I suggest that's enough," he said coldly.

Harrison spun toward Doc, or at least tried to. Doc was not a big man, not in the way Raider was big, but he knew how to use what he had. Keeping a relaxed but firm grip on Harrison's arm while executing minute shifts of his body weight, he used his own balance to keep Harrison from fully regaining his own. Harrison struggled for a few seconds to free his arm, or to get into position to kick out at Doc, and then, as if realizing he was at a disadvantage and only making himself look foolish, he suddenly stopped struggling. The two men stood face to face, staring coldly into one another's eyes.

"I won't forget this, stranger," Harrison said softly. Then, finally tearing his arm free, he turned and walked quickly away.

Doc felt a touch on his arm and started to spin, but it was only Kitty. He saw that she was pale and that she was looking after the retreating Harrison. "You've made yourself a bad enemy," she said.

"I'd rather have him for an enemy than for a friend," Doc replied. "Come on, let's do something for these men."

But other miners were already pouring out of the saloon, bending over their fallen comrades.

"They'll be all right," Kitty said, tugging at Doc's arm. "Let's go to my place before anything else happens. This town..."

The girl suddenly seemed less joyful. How much violence had she seen in this half-wild mining camp? How much of it had she herself suffered? Doc put his arm around her shoulder. "You're right," he said. "If we're going to do battle, let's do it with a champagne bottle."

She smiled. "And I have just the field of battle picked out."

"I'll bet," he replied with an answering smile, thinking of the girl's big bed.

CHAPTER TEN

Raider's first night in Leadville was somewhat less pleasant than Doc's. He'd been signed up by the mine hiring agent and was ready to leave the hiring office when a man, a big man, a miner by his dress, came in. "Got you another live one, Hendry," the hiring agent said.

The big man looked surprised. "Hell, I don't need another man. Got a full crew."

"Head office says you need some more people. Your production's way down."

"Course it's down," Hendry snarled. "Ain't nobody to take the ore up nights. We just dig it out and store it up. And besides, I like to hire my own men."

"Yeah, you've had a pretty free hand so far, Hendry. But head office says *we* hire from now on."

Hendry stared at the hiring agent for a few seconds, then gave Raider a long appraising look. "Okay, so I got me a new man," he snapped. "Be down at the pit head in an hour."

"But Hendry," the hiring agent protested, "he just got into town. He needs a good night's rest."

"Fuck you," Hendry said to the agent. "You say I need a new man, then I must need him now." He turned back to Raider. "You up to it or not, tenderfoot?"

"I'll be there," Raider said flatly.

Hendry continued looking at him for a few more seconds with no appreciable interest in friendliness. Then he turned and stalked out of the office, slamming the door behind him.

"Nice fella," Raider said to the hiring agent. "Who the hell is he, anyhow?"

"Name's Hendry. Foreman of the night shift."

"Is he always this friendly?"

"Meanest man I ever met. Not too many men want to work the night shift. That's kinda helped him have his way, but I guess the company's cracking down a bit. Sure don't envy you, going right down the shaft without a chance to get your bearings."

Raider shrugged. "More money in my pocket. That's what I came up here for. Four dollars a day diggin' rock beats thirty a month punchin' cattle."

The agent scratched his chin. "Well, I dunno. You gotta pay for your own room and board here. And it ain't so nice down the hole. Ah, hell—you'll find out quick enough."

So, with these cheerful words in mind, Raider proceeded to the rooming house the agent had directed him to, stowed his gear in the bare little room he was allotted, had time to put down a quick meal, and then he was off to the pit head. It was a matter of walking; most of the mines were very close to the town. It wasn't a pleasant walk for Raider. He hated working nights, but McParland had figured out that if there was going to be any hanky-panky it would be at night. That didn't make it any easier to slog past the brightly lit saloons and sporting houses, watching all those people having all that fun, while he was off to bust his back. Raider was passing State Street when he saw Doc walking along the boardwalk with as lovely a piece on his arm as Raider had ever seen. Raider ground his teeth. The little bastard had all the luck. Just because he wore all those fancy clothes and had been to college. Ah, shit. The next time he got

Doc out into the boondocks, he was going to run him half to death.

Raider formed up with the rest of Hendry's crew. Damned mean-looking bunch, he thought.

"Well, well. Here's the new boy," Hendry said, grinning, as Raider walked up. "Tonight he's gonna find out what mining's all about, ain't he, boys?"

There was a burst of snickering from the other men. One of them, an enormous barrel-chested ox with forearms the size of Raider's legs, stepped in front of him. "Ain't no doubt we got us a greenhorn here," he said, shoving his forefinger painfully against Raider's chest. Raider felt his temper rising. A good kick in the balls . . . But, no, he was here to do a job for the agency, not get fired before he even had a chance to get started.

If this mountain of muscle in front of him would give him a chance. He was steadily pushing his finger against Raider's chest, driving him backward toward the open pit.

"Give him a quick ride down, Klute," one of the men guffawed.

Raider realized he was going to have to do something to avoid taking a dive down the mine shaft. Hendry didn't look like he was going to do anything to help. It would undoubtedly have ended up in a fight if the mine supervisor, seeing the men standing there, hadn't shouted, "Get those men down the shaft, Hendry. We ain't payin' 'em to look at the stars."

Hendry swore under his breath, then snarled, "Okay, Klute, let him be. Everybody down the shaft."

A big steam engine was chugging away next to the pit head. It provided power for the cage lift. The crew filed inside, and almost immediately the cage began to descend. It only required one trip for the entire crew, because it numbered only a dozen men. When McParland had briefed Raider and Doc, he'd explained that in this mine, only a skeleton crew worked the night shift.

To Raider, the cage seemed to go down forever. The only light came from the lanterns they all carried, and around them, endless blackness.

One of the men sensed Raider's uneasiness. "This here's one o' the deepest shafts in Leadville," he chuckled. "Been worked a long time. Probably just about worked out."

The farther they descended, the hotter the air grew. And the fouler. Raider was already having trouble breathing, and he hadn't even started working yet. He was grateful when the cage finally touched bottom. They had passed other gallery openings on the way down, and as he stepped out of the cage, Raider saw tunnels running off in several directions.

Raider was led off into a small gallery where he could barely stand erect because the roof was so low. Wet rock glistened all around. The temperature had to be at least ninety degrees, and it was very humid. The gallery ended at a face of crumbly blue rock.

"We're startin' you easy, new boy," Hendry growled. "Just dig out that blue stuff—that's carbonate of lead, stuff's fulla silver—put it in the wheelbarrow, an' dump it in a pile out there in the main gallery."

"I'm workin' all alone?" Raider asked.

"Hell yes. Hope you ain't afraid o' the dark."

Klute was standing behind Hendry, and he guffawed loudly. Raider looked up at the big man. You'll get yours sooner or later, asshole, Raider promised himself.

Hendry was saying, "This here's your canary an' your candle. If the candle starts to go out, then you ain't got no oxygen left, and you better try and make it to the cage. An' if your canary dies, then there's gas so you'd better douse your light before the whole place blows. Anyhow, start diggin'. You get a rest break in three hours."

And with that, Hendry and Klute turned and left, leaving Raider alone in the small tunnel, which did nothing for his incipient claustrophobia. He looked over at his caged canary and carefully studied the light from the candle flame, certain that he was already suffocating. To take his mind off it he began working. Turning to face the ore seam, he started chipping loose the soft crumbly ore with his pick and digging bar, then shoveling it into the wheelbarrow. No need for drilling and blasting here. Just grunt work. And here he was, working for four bucks a day, digging out a fortune in silver ore for some rich bastard like Tabor. Hell, it *was* for Tabor.

Raider worked for hours without doing much thinking. The digging was somewhat hypnotic: just dig, dig, dig, shovel, shovel, shovel, then, as a kind of break, run the loaded wheelbarrow back down the tunnel and dump it in the main shaft.

On about his tenth load, Raider, after dumping the wheel-barrow, stopped for a moment to rest. There was no one in sight, just darkness all around, although he thought he could see a faint gleam of light way off down one tunnel. And he could hear sounds—not the sounds of drilling or digging, which he would have expected from a working mine, but something that sounded more or less like iron wheels running slowly over an iron track.

Nobody had come after what Raider figured was three hours, so he took his own break, munching some food he'd brought down the shaft. A couple of hours later one of the men showed up.

"Lunchtime," he informed Raider. To Raider's surprise, the man pulled out his lunch, sat down on a rock shelf, and began to eat.

"We ain't joinin' the others?" Raider asked.

"Naw. They're off workin' another face."

Raider said nothing, just sat down and started to eat. The man had brought a huge container of water, which Raider was glad of, because he'd long ago run through what he had with him. It was so hot and humid that he'd sweated most of the moisture in him right through his clothes.

Raider suspected the man was as much there to watch him as to keep him company. Raider's suspicions were reinforced when, after Raider suggested it might be a nice idea to stretch his legs a little, the man hurriedly tried to get him to change his mind.

"This is a hell of a dangerous place if'n you ain't used to it," he insisted. "You could fall down a shaft, maybe go in someplace where the roof's rotten and start a cave-in, or maybe just find bad air and kinda choke to death."

"Well, I'll never learn the layout if I don't move around a little."

"That don't make no difference," the man said sullenly. "You gotta stay here. I'm responsible for you. Yes sirree, this would be one hell of a place to get lost in."

Raider let it drop. He'd have plenty of time in the future to start nosing around. Right at the moment, the most important thing was to get through the shift. The work, combined with the fact that he hadn't slept for two days, already had his muscles aching from head to foot, and the heat and foul air were making him nauseous. When his lunch break was over he started working doggedly at the ore face again.

The other man watched for a while. Then, as if satisfied that Raider wasn't going anywhere, he disappeared into the darkness, the light of his lantern seeming to snuff out as he turned a corner.

By the time the shift was over, Raider was exhausted. The others picked him up on their way back to the cage. They seemed tired too. Most of them were covered with sticky bluish ore dust, which indicated that they'd certainly been working at *something*.

It was early morning when they filed out of the cage into the open air. Raider was enormously relieved to have the sky, rather than a rock ceiling, over him again. Beyond that, he had no more complicated desires than a hot bath, a thick steak, a few quarts of cool wet beer, and then about ten hours' sleep.

Then he was suddenly alert. Something was wrong, something out of place. It took him a few seconds to realize what had bothered him. Several of the men, including Hendry and Klute, had burrs and bits of brush clinging to their clothing, mixed in with the blue smear of ore dust. But how? He hadn't heard the cage going up the shaft, and he'd have had to hear it from where he'd been working, so either plants were growing at the bottom of the mine shaft or some of the men had been outside by some other route.

Raider chewed this problem over all through his bath,

through the enormous meal he ate, and the beers he washed the food down with. But it wasn't enough to keep him from falling asleep seconds after he flopped down onto his narrow cot and pulled the blankets around himself.

When he awoke later in the afternoon, Raider was almost too stiff and sore to get out of bed. Groaning, he dressed, then ate, which helped his mood, then visited one of the town saloons for a few beers, which loosened him up even more. By the time the night shift started, Raider was feeling halfway human.

The heat in the mines actually helped, loosening his muscles, so that Raider had little difficulty chipping away once again at the ore face in that narrow, solitary little tunnel. Once again, mid-shift, his companion-guard showed up, keeping an eye on him while he ate. Now, more than ever, Raider was certain there was something out of the ordinary going on in the mine during the night shift, even if it was only a floating crap game. But what did those weeds mean, stuck to the clothing of the men the night before?

When the shift ended and the crew climbed, blinking, into the bright light of day, Raider noticed nothing out of the ordinary. Klute tried to trip him when he stepped out of the lift cage, but Raider managed instead to grind his boot heel into the bigger man's instep. Klute hopped around on one foot, calling Raider every obscenity in the book. Raider looked coldly into Klute's eyes, which quieted the other man for a moment.

"The next time, my boot goes up your ass," Raider said in a deadly voice, and while Klute was still mulling that one over, he walked away.

Raider went straight into the center of town. He'd already been informed which room at the Clarendon was Doc's, and, slipping in through the back entrance, he went quietly and rapidly up the stairs. There was no one in the hallway outside Doc's room, so Raider knocked lightly. Nothing happened. He knocked a little more loudly. This time there was a faint grunt from within.

"Goddamn it, you little bastard!" Raider finally snarled,

giving the door a hearty kick with his muddy boot. "Open the fucking door!"

A moment's silence, then footsteps padded toward the door, a bolt slid back, and the door opened a crack. But Doc was nowhere in sight. When Raider pushed his way into the room, there was his partner, behind the door, wearing a beautiful silk dressing gown, blinking at him bleary-eyed, and holding his Colt Lightning in one hand.

"Nervous?" Raider snorted, indicating the pistol.

"It sounded like an army was about to come charging through my door," Doc muttered grumpily, wiping sleep from his eyes.

"Guess that's what it'd take to get a city slicker like you outta the rack." His eyes traveled around the ornate room. "So this is how the other half lives."

Doc stumbled over and looked at his watch, which was lying next to the bed on a beautiful little inlaid table. "My God, it's still the middle of the night!"

"Sun's been up for near on half an hour," Raider snapped. "Time things got moving around here."

"Sure . . . sure," Doc muttered. "It was a late night for me, that's all."

"A late night for *you?*" Raider hooted, remembering his twelve hours below ground.

Not having a suitable reply for that, Doc changed the subject. "You're getting mud all over the carpets," he groused. "My *god* but you smell! Don't you ever take a bath?"

"Look, you little shit," Raider snarled, reaching out one big pick-blistered hand and picking Doc up by the front of his dressing gown, lifting him six inches off the floor. "I've had a hard couple of days, and I ain't got time for any o' your damned nagging. Now, how you makin' out? Or do I have to ask?"

It didn't help Raider's mood that the necks of two empty champagne bottles were protruding from an ice bucket placed conveniently near the bed. Or that some undecipherable but obviously intimate article of a woman's wearing apparel was lying on the carpet, undoubtedly discarded in haste.

Doc, sensing this was probably not a good time to push back, gently disengaged his dressing gown from Raider's grimy paw.

"I'm working on the woman...Baby Doe," he said. "I have an appointment with her tomorrow morning, in my guise as a doctor. I am, as you might put it, working on this thing from the very top."

"While I'm sure as hell way down at the bottom," Raider grunted. "And that damned mine is sure to God the bottom of hell. I don't know how them damn miners do it, year in and year out. I wouldn't do that kinda work for a hundred bucks a day."

"Rough, huh?" Doc said diplomatically.

"Rougher'n a concrete corncob 'gainst a virgin's ass. But I think I may be onto something. There's strange things happenin' down in that miserable pit."

He went on to tell Doc about Hendry and the seeming lack of normal mine-working procedure, and about the hostility of the men to his presence on their shift. "I'm gonna make a play tonight," he said. "See what I can find out. They're fallin' into a routine with me, so I can work around the edges of their timing."

Doc was, on the one hand, a bit worried about his partner sticking his neck out, and on the other, a bit upset that things seemed to be developing so quickly. He'd had another fine night with Kitty, and was looking forward to many more. She was getting to the point where she was refusing to charge him for her favors, which only reinforced Doc's suspicions that the girl didn't have the necessary hardness to survive in this kind of environment. He was worried about her.

Raider was already on his way out the door, his filthy boots leaving telltale signs of his passing. Doc wondered what the hotel staff was going to think. Raider turned at the door for one final word. "That little piece of fluff I saw you with the other night," he said. "When this damned thing is over, I'm gonna want some o' that."

"Raider," Doc spluttered angrily. "You can take your goddamned wants and shove them."

"Come off it, Doc. She didn't look like no virgin to me. More like a bride o' the multitude."

And, satisfied that he had left his easy-living partner in a suitable state of mental disruption, Raider headed home for a bath and his bed.

When he showed up for work that night, his fellow miners seemed, if anything, even more resentful of his presence. Not wanting to foul up his plans, Raider paid no attention to Klute's steady stream of insults. Clearly the big man was trying to goad him into a fight. Raider stayed out of his way, and once the cage reached the bottom of the shaft, he went off by himself to chip docilely away at his ore face.

But after an hour had passed, Raider, knowing that if all went the same as on the previous two days, no one would come looking for him for quite a while, dropped his tools and slipped out into the main tunnel. As before, all was dark, except for the faint beam of light coming from one of the side tunnels. Leaving his lantern behind, he stepped boldly into that other tunnel and began moving slowly along it, feeling his way by sweeping a length of wood ahead of him like a blind man's cane. The faint light ahead helped, and the farther he went, the stronger it became. Finally he leaned his piece of wood up against the side of the tunnel and, keeping close to one side, peered around a corner.

An enormous cavern lay beyond. Obviously the seam of silver-bearing ore had widened considerably here. To shore up this vast space, the engineers had used Diedesheimer square sets, which consisted of interlocking frames of twelve-by-twelve timbers, reaching clear to the roof.

The rest of the night crew was busily at work. The mouth of another tunnel lay open, and out of it ran a pair of metal rails. Raider watched the crew, under Hendry's direction, loading ore cars, then trundling them into the tunnel's mouth.

"Okay," he heard Hendry call out. "Let's take a break."

Raider hoped this didn't mean they were going to send a man to take a break with him, but to his relief they all sat down around a half-loaded ore car. Klute produced and passed around a half-full bottle of whiskey. It was quite a scene of relaxation—except for the conversation.

"I'm gettin' more and more nervous about that new man," Hendry said. "That's the first time they ever forced anybody on me."

"Think he's a plant?"

"Could be. And if he is, I don't know how long I can keep him buried off on his own."

Klute took a healthy swig from the whiskey bottle, then wiped his mouth with the back of one huge hand. "Maybe the thing to do is bury him permanently."

"As a last resort," Hendry said. "If he's a plant, then they'll know something's wrong for sure. But the longer he stays, the more he slows us down. Another month, that's all we need, then we'll be set for life, every man jack of us."

"Maybe our new mate could have himself a little accident," one of the men mused. "You know—fall down some stairs, or get stepped on by a horse. Just enough to keep him from workin'."

Klute casually tossed the empty bottle behind him, where it shattered against the side of an ore car. "Don't have to be no accident," he said. "Don't have to hide it, neither."

"What the hell you up to, Klute," Hendry demanded.

Klute grinned, an action that, to Raider, made the big man look like a constipated ape. "Leave it to me," Klute said, grinning. "When the shift's over and we're up top, it's just gonna be two good old boys havin' themselves a little misunderstanding."

"Okay," Hendry said worriedly. "But don't kill him, Klute. Just bust him up a little so's he can't work."

"I'll tie his arms together in a bow knot an' wrap his legs around his neck," Klute said, still grinning. "And when I'm finished, you can fire him for fightin'."

The men were making the motions of getting back to work, so Raider, remembering to pick up his stick, groped his way hurriedly back to his tunnel. When his guardian showed up sometime later, he was industriously picking away at his ore face.

The rest of the day dragged for Raider. He knew he probably couldn't avoid a showdown with Klute. The im-

portant thing was to cover his back. Of course, he could
always hightail it out, but he doubted he'd have the chance.
And besides, he needed another day's access to the mine.
So when the shift ended and they were once again on their
way up to a world of light, Raider watched Klute carefully.
To his surprise, the big man appeared unusually amiable,
smiling and whistling through his teeth on the long way up.

Once they were on the surface, Klute approached him.
"The rest of us are gonna go have a drink or two. Why
don't ya come along?"

Raider nodded acceptance, trying not to show hesitation.
If there had to be a showdown, better to have it in a public
place.

Despite the early hour, the saloon they entered was doing
a roaring business. Hendry's crew of a dozen men lined up
at the bar and ordered their poison. It was the liveliest Raider
had ever seen them. They were laughing and joking as if
they were at a circus, grinning expectantly at Raider and
Klute.

As for Klute, he was pouring down the alcohol, not for
courage, Raider suspected, but simply because he liked to
drink. Or perhaps to make it look like he'd gotten drunk
and didn't know what he was doing.

The big man finally turned and walked over to Raider,
a large whiskey in one huge paw. "You stepped on my foot
yesterday," he said, grinning.

"Reckon as I did," Raider replied amiably.

"But you was too yella-bellied to stick around and talk
about it."

"I don't have time to stop and talk about every piece of
dog shit I step on," Raider said quietly, but his voice carried,
and now most of the men in the saloon knew that a fight
was brewing. Seeing that big Klute was one of the princi-
pals, ears pricked up.

Klute tried to keep the grin on his face, but he was having
a difficult time. "You're callin' me dog shit, ain't you?" he
asked tightly.

"Sorry if I'm usin' words too big for your little pea
brain," Raider said.

Both he and Klute were standing next to the bar, about six feet apart. Smiling again, Klute reached out and poured his whiskey over Raider's shirt, standing solid, expecting Raider to throw a punch, but when Raider made no move, just continued to lean lightly against the bar, Klute sneered. "Yella, just like I thought," he said. "But it ain't gonna help you none, big-mouth, 'cause I don't like people callin' me dog shit."

He turned to put his glass on the bar, still standing solid, legs braced, squarely in front of Raider. As soon as he started to turn around again, Raider wound up with all he had and kicked the bigger man square in the crotch.

"Aauuwf!" Klute bellowed, doubling up, his hands dropping toward the source of all that sickening pain. Raider, continuing his forward movement, slammed his fists hard into Klute's face again and again. He knew he stood little chance in a toe-to-toe punch-out with Klute; a man that huge would hammer him right into the floor. It had to be quick, but already it was taking longer than he had expected. His fists were slamming against Klute's face with a sound like an ax thudding into a wet log, but Klute was still on his feet, back-pedaling now, unable to get his hands up to defend himself but proving able to take incredible punishment. Maybe a boot in the gut would help. Anything. Fighting fair with Klute would be like asking for an invitation to your own funeral.

And then someone grabbed Raider from behind. Someone else jerked his legs out from under him and he went down with a third man riding his back. He twisted sideways to avoid a boot aimed at his head. The rest of the night crew was going for him!

The melee grew as other men stepped in. "Let it be a fight between the two of them," a huge drover bellowed, plucking the man from Raider's back.

"But he kicked Klute in the balls," one of the crew shouted.

"A goddamned good shot, too," someone said with a laugh. "Somethin' that big ox's had comin' to him for a long time. Now get the hell out of it and let 'em fight."

Raider was able to get to his feet again, with nothing worse than a rib sore from an enthusiastic boot. The trouble was, Klute had had time to recover. He was standing about eight feet away, shaking his head like an angry bull, looking around for Raider, and when he saw him he charged, head down, bull-like. Raider slammed another couple of blows against Klute's head as he came on, but it was as futile as throwing snowballs at a block of granite. Klute's huge body slammed into him, sending him reeling back. He might have fallen, but Klute's enormous arms wrapped around him, holding him up, but not out of affection. Those arms began to tighted around Raider's ribs, and he knew the big man was capable of snapping his back if he got a good enough hold.

Struggling desperately, Raider smashed the top of his head against Klute's face. Klute loosened his grip a little. Raider reached behind his back and, seizing one of Klute's fingers, bent it back as far as he could. Klute howled with pain and let go for a second. Raider tried to twist out of the way, but Klute's arms closed again, like giant nutcrackers, this time around Raider's neck, immobilizing him in a headlock.

Klute began to grunt and strain, trying to twist Raider's neck around. Their faces were only inches apart, Klute's eyes glaring into Raider's, red, like the eyes of a wild pig. Raider knew the big man was going to try to break his neck. He had only seconds left.

Suddenly remembering something Doc had once taught him, something he'd laughed at at the time, Raider managed to get one hand in between his head and Klute's. He fumbled the hand upward, his palm against Klute's mouth, the edge of his hand, the little finger edge, making contact with the base of Klute's nose.

Raider pushed up remorselessly. Klute tried to struggle, but the septum of the nose is one of the weakest and most sensitive parts of the body. Klute's head was forced further and further back, weakening his headlock. Suddenly Raider was free, with Klute bent partway backward. Raider slammed his fist into Klute's belly. Normally it would have been like hitting a tree trunk, but with Klute's abdominal muscles stretched and open, the blow went deep into the diaphragm. Klute wheezed and bent forward, temporarily out of air.

That was one of the first signs Raider had seen that Klute was human. He could be hurt, but hitting that rocklike head was a waste of time, so Raider's next two blows went to Klute's kidneys. Klute had too little air left to scream, but his legs began to buckle.

Raider slammed a knee into Klute's ribs. He heard one of them snap. He continued raining blows to the big man's body, driving him lower and lower, but Klute seemed to hate the idea of going down. He ended up squatting, bent forward, the back of his thick neck bulging above the dirty collar of his shirt. Clasping his hands together, Raider slammed their combined edges down against that thick neck, blow after blow, until at last, with a soft sigh, Klute collapsed forward onto his face.

For a few seconds you could have heard a pin drop in the saloon, then cheers broke from most of the onlookers, with the exception of Hendry's crew, of course.

"Looks like you could use a drink, stranger," one of the men at the bar said. A moment later Raider's hand was filled by a glass. He tossed down the harsh whiskey, shuddering at the bite of it, but it helped steady his breathing. Friendly hands guided him to the bar. He leaned against it wearily. Fighting Klute had been as exhausting as a twelve-hour shift down the hole.

While Raider was being feted by the miners, Hendry's crew picked up Klute. Two men, wheezing from the weight, dragged the big man out of the saloon, his arms slung over their shoulders, his head sagging, his boot heels carving trails through the dirty sawdust that littered the saloon's floor.

Hendry looked over at Raider for a moment. "You're fired," he said flatly, then followed his men out through the swinging doors.

For another quarter of an hour Raider accepted the hospitality being offered him, then, pleading sore ribs, he worked his way through well-wishers until he was once again outside. "Gotta get some sleep, boys," he said, and they cheered him. But once out of sight of the saloon, Raider headed not for his rooming house but for the mine.

He got to the pit head just as a load of day-shift miners were filing into the cage. The day-shift crews were much larger than the night shift, and his presence among them occasioned no comment.

Once at the bottom, Raider quickly oriented himself and located the entrance to the tunnel where he'd been working for the past three days. It was easy from there to find the other tunnel, the one that led into the big gallery. The place was full of light and movement now, with miners busy everywhere, but when Raider entered that huge gallery with the Diedesheimer square set shoring, he looked around in confusion. Where the hell were the tracks that Hendry and the others had been using to carry their ore cars?

There was nothing at all on the floor of the big cavern. It looked to be just what it was—a vein worked out long ago and now only a passageway. Nor could Raider find the tunnel Hendry and his boys had been so busily rolling ore cars into. There was nothing along the walls but stacks of shoring lumber and other mining material.

At first Raider thought he must have wandered into the wrong part of the mine, but then the obvious occurred to him. Lining himself up with the entrance of the tunnel from which he'd just exited, he walked over and peered behind one of the big piles of shoring timbers and equipment. Sure enough, there *was* a tunnel entrance, not completely hidden, which would have looked suspicious to those who knew a tunnel belonged there, but well enough concealed to put it out of everyone's mind. Except for Hendry and his crew.

When Raider asked a passing miner about the tunnel, the miner merely said it was an old, worked-out gallery. Raider waited until the man was out of sight, no one else near, then quickly wormed his way behind the stack of material and slid into the dark hole of the half-hidden tunnel mouth.

His lantern only cast light for a short way; the inky blackness swallowed it up. About forty yards inside the tunnel, Raider found a stack of rails, just enough to reach out into the big gallery. Hendry's crew, then, must lay the rails down anew each night, out into the gallery. From where Raider now stood, more permanent-looking rails curved off into the tunnel's blackness. Raider followed, the light from his lantern gleaming faintly off the track, the metal well polished from constant use. He walked on and on, amazed at the length of the tunnel, but he'd heard that some of the ore seams reached deep into the mountain.

Finally, Raider reached the spot where the ore seam had petered out. But the tunnel didn't end there. He saw signs of more recent digging, obviously through non-ore-bearing rock. By now he could feel a faint flow of air against his face. Fresh air. It was only a little farther down this new stretch of digging that the tunnel ended—and not at a blank face.

The air was cold now, and Raider could smell plants and moist earth. He had to push aside a wooden screen, and then ahead he saw bright light. Another few yards and he was standing in a little gully, in which the tunnel entrance seemed to be no more than a dark cleft in a rocky fold. Proceeding cautiously—there might be guards—Raider walked down the gully and all at once found himself on the side of a mountain. A quick check of the view told Raider that he was probably on the far side of the mountain from the mine entrance. The ground outside the gully had been churned up by wagon wheels. A well-used road lay only fifty yards away. Stepping out onto the road, Raider saw a stamp mill about a half mile further along. Clever. Take the ore out through the unused tunnel, which they had cut through to the outside, then transfer it to wagons and haul it to the mill, *if* the mill ahead was the one Hendry and his bunch were using.

Rather than go back into the mine, Raider cut over the nearest ridge, heading back for town. He had an earful for Doc.

CHAPTER ELEVEN

Earlier that morning, Doc had kept his appointment with Baby Doe, Tabor's lady love. In the short time he'd been in Leadville, he'd managed to make a quick reputation as a fashionable man of medicine, catering to the rich ladies of the town, always solicitous of their ills, real or imagined. His natural bedside manner had nearly gotten him under the covers with more than one of these bored, pampered pets of the mining aristocracy, but he'd held back, not from shyness, but because he knew from past experience that such an action would limit his access to the company of those who had not yet sampled him. The word of it would get around fast, and then some of his mystery, the mystery of unavailability, would have dispersed, especially that titillation of knowing that, while he was obviously a virile man, he was also safe to be alone with. In other words, the Hairdresser Syndrome.

Doc went up the stairs to Baby Doe's suite in the Hotel Vendome, which Tabor had built expressly for her. Like most of the dwellings of the time, the suite was incredibly cluttered with heavy, overstuffed furniture and endless bric-a-brac. A maid showed Doc in, then left. He set down his leather gladstone, filled with his homeopathic medicines, on a thick, obviously very expensive oriental carpet next to an inlaid coffee table. He was lost in thought for a moment, pondering the vast distances the various objects in the room must have traveled.

Then Baby Doe came into the room, a regal entrance, although not at all an arrogant one. Baby Doe simply moved with an intrinsic grace and sureness, as if she'd known all her life what she wanted and it was only right that she should now have it.

"Dr. Weatherbee?" she asked in a slightly husky contralto.

"At your service, ma'am," Doc replied, executing a slight bow.

"I'm so glad you could come," she said. She was about to say something more but hesitated.

"Is there some specific problem?" Doc asked.

Baby Doe looked at him for a moment, her enormous eyes awing Doc. "No, there's nothing *really* specific," she finally said. "But sometimes I...I seem to have a little trouble breathing, and...and"—she placed her right hand over her magnificent breasts—"I feel a tightness here."

Doc was feeling a vague tightness himself, partly in his throat, partly much lower in his body. Baby Doe was wearing a long peignoir made of rose-colored silk, and underneath that rather insubstantial garment was one hell of a lot of woman. When she placed her hand on her breasts, they pressed inward with an appearance of marvelous resiliency.

"You...you don't think it could be my heart, do you?" Baby Doe asked hesitantly.

"That is certainly something we can check," Doc replied. "If you would like to sit in that chair...."

Baby Doe sat down in the indicated chair. Doc went over to her, and bending down, looked into her eyes, which he noticed were amazingly clear. She looked back up at him trustingly. Or was it more than that? He realized quite acutely that he was in the company of one of the most naturally sensual women he'd ever met. He was aware of an odor of musk, of what seemed to be sexual excitement emanating from her body. Did she want to make love to him? That would be an interesting development. If she was ready to cheat Tabor sexually, perhaps she would not hesitate to cheat him in other ways.

Doc leaned closer and put his ear against Baby Doe's chest, so that he could listen to her heart and lungs. Unselfconsciously, she parted the top of her peignoir to make it easier for him. The side of his face made contact with the warm pliant flesh of Baby Doe's magnificent breasts. He was so aware of the femaleness of her that for a moment he forgot to listen to her breathing and the steady, strong beat of her heart. A very steady beat. No sign of unusual excitement at all.

Doc pulled back to look at Baby Doe, who was providing him with a very lovely view, with her peignoir pulled down nearly free of her breasts, only the nipples hidden, but noticeable beneath the thin material. Lower down, the peignoir had slipped partially free of her legs, baring a good deal of one lovely thigh.

"Well, Dr. Weatherbee?" Baby Doe asked in that marvelously sexy contralto. "How am I?"

Doc wanted to say, "All that a man could desire," but wisely refrained. It was dawning on him that Baby Doe was not making a play for him at all. The sexual aura that emanated from the woman was simply natural to her, like the timbre of her voice. Lucky devil, Tabor.

Doc made a few more examinations, including taking her pulse, pondered a while, quite professional now, forgetting for the moment his role of spy. Finally he stepped back. "As far as I can see, young woman, you are an amazingly healthy human being."

"Oh?" she said, obviously pleased, as most people are when they hear such a statement, but Doc noticed a small hesitation, which she quickly put into words. "And the shortness of breath? The tightness in my chest?"

Doc looked more closely, saw the slight tension behind those fine warm eyes. "I think that something is bothering you," he said bluntly. "Something connected with your personal life rather than your body."

She looked a little flustered. "Ah . . . yes."

"Of course, emotional stress is quite capable of manifesting itself physically, and if the stress continues long enough, that fine healthy body of yours may cease to be so healthy."

"It . . . *is* so very stressful," she murmured, looking slightly to one side.

"It might be better for you if you could unload some of that stress," Doc said, looking straight at Baby Doe now, willing her eyes to meet his.

She looked up at him questioningly, seeing at that moment a father confessor, unaware of the spy. "It's . . . it's something that's happening with my . . . with Horace," she burst out.

"Uh-huh," Doc said reassuringly as he sat down in front of her.

"It's . . . it's our situation . . . his wife," Baby Doe continued in a low tense voice. "Of course, we're not married. Well, yes we are, but . . . but, it's all such a terrible mess."

It all came pouring out, Doc wisely keeping his mouth shut most of the time, merely prompting her by extending sympathy and understanding. He was, of course, collecting information vital to his case, but was also extending real relief, by giving Baby Doe a chance to talk out her troubles in front of a neutral, safe audience.

It turned out that Augusta, Tabor's wife, had been asking for separate maintenance for some time, as McParland had noted. But there were many things McParland didn't know. For instance, that Bill Bush, a good friend of Tabor's, had been acting as an emissary on Tabor's behalf, asking Augusta to grant Tabor a divorce. Augusta had refused, several times.

And now, increasingly interesting revelations from Baby Doe, which had Doc on the edge of his seat. During the summer Tabor had made a trip to Durango, down in the southwest corner of the state, where he had some landholdings, and had gotten his friends in the local judiciary to grant him a secret divorce from Augusta. And an even more interesting revelation: During a trip to Saint Louis, Tabor had just as secretly married Baby Doe.

That was all very nice, Tabor's lawyers had informed him, but since Augusta had not been informed of the Durango divorce, it was not legal, and it could be argued, legally, that Tabor now had two wives. In short, that he was a bigamist. "We could find some way to live with that," Baby Doe said sadly. "But it's this Senate thing. Horace *so* wants to be a senator, and if the news ever got out . . . well, people out here are pretty liberal, but they're never going to elect a bigamist to the United States Senate."

"Yes . . . I see," Doc murmured, reflecting on the difficulties of the life of a silver millionaire.

"But we're trying to get Augusta to agree to a divorce before the election," Baby Doe continued. "Horace is offering her an awful lot of money, and the house in Denver. Horace is trying as hard as he can to convince her."

Yes, undoubtedly he was, Doc thought. A man as rich as Tabor, and with so much influence in Colorado, just might be able to force his overmatched wife to do as he wanted. But that was not Doc's worry. There was a matter of some missing silver.

"You care very much what happens to Mr. Tabor, don't you?" he abruptly asked, cutting into Baby Doe's sad soliloquy.

She blinked her huge warm eyes. "I'd do anything for him," she said simply. "Horace is my whole life."

Doc believed her. This lovely, sensual woman was not the source of Tabor's losses. She was just what she seemed to be on the surface—nothing hidden, nothing tricky, an honest woman concerned about her man. Yes, she was also wedded to pleasure and luxury, but so what? Doc liked luxury too.

There was not much more to the interview. Doc reassured Baby Doe. "I've heard that Mr. Tabor can move mountains when he wants to. And, while he may want the Senate seat very badly, I have no doubt that he also must realize that the company of such a woman as yourself is far more important than any social honor."

Well, that was laying it on a bit thickly, but Doc's high-flown words seemed to have the desired effect. When he left, Baby Doe was glowing with exuberance. She'd forgotten to fasten the top of her peignoir, and, as Doc stood in the doorway saying goodbye, she moved in front of a window and the bright light from outside clearly outlined the richness of her body through the material. Doc closed the door regretfully, and as he went down the stairs all he could think was, Oh, that lucky bastard, Tabor.

CHAPTER TWELVE

When Doc got back to his room, he discovered Raider already there, pacing the floor impatiently. "Where the hell you been?" Raider demanded.

"With Baby Doe. Looking for information."

"Huh? Yeah, I'll bet."

"Watch your mouth!" Doc exploded. "She's a fine woman."

Raider looked speculatively at Doc. "Made an impression on you, did she?"

"She did. I have no doubt she's totally loyal to Tabor. In all ways," he added pointedly.

"Glad to hear you like the lady. But she don't matter no more anyhow. I found out who's been stealin' the silver . . . and how they been doin' it."

Doc's eyebrows went up. "Well, well. I suppose sometimes the simple approach . . ."

Raider glowered at his partner, then proceeded to recount his discoveries.

"Amazing," Doc broke in, "that they could have gotten away with it for so long."

"Yeah. Nobody blabbermouthed, which is somethin'. 'Course, I guess Hendry coulda turned Klute onto 'em anytime, which would help keep the troops in line. Still, to find a whole crew . . ."

"I'm certain the potential rewards must have helped," Doc said. "They must have taken out one hell of a lot of silver. Depends on how long they've been at it. The question is, what do we do now?"

"Yeah. I guess the only thing we can do is stake out that gully and wait for 'em to make their next move. I know they don't cart the ore outta the mine every night. They must keep squirreling it away until they get enough to make a run. If there was only some way . . . Hey! There's Hendry, down in the alley, talkin' to some dude."

Raider had wandered over to the window while he was talking, not really looking for anything, but sure enough, there was Hendry, standing behind the corner of a building, leaning tensely toward another man. Raider could see that both men were talking vehemently, but of course, he couldn't make out the words.

Doc crowded next to him. "That's Hendry?" he asked. "The thickset one?"

"Yeah. But I don't know the other man."

"I do. His name's Harrison. Jack Harrison." Doc looked up at Raider and grinned. "He's an enemy of Tabor's . . . and he owns a stamp mill."

"Well, I'll be damned," Raider said. "An' I've got an idea I know just where that mill is."

"I saw those two talking in an alley the other night," Doc said. "The first night you went down into the mine."

"And I'm pretty sure they took a load out that night. So maybe tonight . . ."

"A damned good chance. Now, let's figure what to do about it."

In the end, they had no choice but to go to Tabor. Since the action was probably scheduled for tonight, there was no way they could contact McParland and get reinforcements in time. Using McParland's name, they gained access to Tabor, who was in his office.

"So you're the ones McParland sent," Tabor said. He looked more closely at Doc. "I know you...seen you around."

"I'm sure you have, Mr. Tabor," Doc said. "We've both been in town several days." If Tabor found out he'd been spying on Baby Doe...

"And you've cracked this thing already?" Tabor asked unbelievingly.

While Tabor sat behind his desk, looking even more walrus-like than usual, with his enormous mustache and bulging eyes, Doc gave him the story. Tabor took the first part calmly enough, about Hendry and his crew of thieves working in Tabor's very own mine, but when Harrison's name came up, Tabor exploded.

"That son of a bitch!" he bellowed. "I'm gonna string that bastard up to the nearest lamppost!"

"Well, we haven't actually caught him at it yet."

"Don't matter. I'm gonna call out my troops and go over there and burn his damned mill down to the ground, with him in it."

Raider was leaning back against the wall, grinning. Tabor was his kind of man, a believer in direct action. No pussy-footing around with lawyers and courts and all that folderol.

Doc, however, was not about to give in. "If you do that," he insisted stiffly, "if you act without any evidence, and believe me, most of what we have so far is conjecture, then there could be a lot of trouble."

"I ain't scared o' trouble," Tabor snarled.

"There could be endless lawsuits. Once the lawyers get into it..."

Tabor began to look worried. "Uh-huh. Well, I *am* scared o' lawyers. Damned slippery, lyin', thievin' bastards."

"Exactly. Why act precipitately, then, when all we have to do is wait a few hours and catch them in the act? We're pretty certain they're going to run a load of ore out tonight.

Run it straight to Harrison's mill, no doubt. I repeat: All we have to do is wait."

"But we ain't got the men," Raider cut in. "There's gonna be a helluva lot of them, and believe me, they're tough customers."

"That's our problem," Doc said to Tabor. "We'll never get a wire to McParland in time to receive reinforcements."

"Damn it! Use my telephone!" Tabor bellowed. "What the hell do you think I had the thing put in for?"

Before Doc or Raider could reply, Tabor walked over to the big wooden telephone cabinet affixed to the wall and began vigorously cranking the handle to alert the operator. There was more bellowing as Tabor asked to be put through to McParland in Denver.

There was a considerable wait as the connection was made.

"We could use my Highland Guards, o' course," Tabor said. "Call out the Tabor Light Cavalry, too, for that matter."

Then the connection was made.

"McParland?" Tabor yelled into the mouthpiece. "Tabor here. Hold on for a moment."

He held out the phone to Doc, who took charge of the instrument with apparent ease, although, in truth, he had rarely used one before. He began telling McParland the situation.

"What's that? Speak up!" McParland's faraway, tinny voice crackled into his ear. Doc talked loudly and briefly, then McParland asked to be connected with Raider.

Raider took the earpiece gingerly, then mashed it tightly against his left ear. He jumped when he heard McParland's voice.

"Are you sure of all this?" McParland demanded.

"Yes, sir!" Raider screamed into the mouthpiece, aware of all that incredible distance separating him from McParland. His body was tense and his face frozen. He didn't like any of this; it was spooky. Besides, he liked to see a man's eyes when he talked to him.

Finally it was settled. McParland was going to start

rounding up men and put them on the train for Leadville. But he doubted they'd be able to make it there before the next day. For the meantime, he told his two detectives, they should cooperate with Tabor: "It's his money, so he might as well use his own men to get it back."

Tabor talked a while longer while Raider leaned against the wall, his ear still buzzing. After that, it was time to make concrete plans. The plans themselves were quite simple — to stake out the gully where the exit mouth of the illicit tunnel was and see what happened.

Once the final arrangements were made, and the commanders of Tabor's two palace guards called into the office and given their orders, Raider, yawning, told the others he was going back to his room to catch up on his sleep.

Tabor looked admiringly after him as he went out the door. "Got nerves o' steel, that man," he said to the room in general.

"Well, Mr. Tabor," Doc drawled, "he *does* hate to miss his sleep."

Raider seemed to be adequately rested when, that night, about an hour after dark, the forces of law and order moved stealthily into place on the road between the hidden tunnel entrance and Harrison's mill. Tabor had come with forty men, dressed, to Raider's amusement, in their parade ground uniforms.

"Them boys are gonna get burrs in their asses," he chuckled to Doc as the Highland Guards, kilts swinging, marched into place.

The Light Cavalry were posted back about a quarter mile, holding their horses, ready to gallop in at the charge once the infantry had made contact.

It was a dark night, and cold, with a hint of snow in the air. Winter was at hand, and winter was harsh in Leadville. Kitty had told Doc, "There's only three seasons in this damn place — July, August, and winter."

It was difficult keeping Tabor's storybook soldiers quiet and in their places. The gully widened out into a shallow canyon before it reached the road, and there was considerable high ground on each side of the road. Perfect for the ambush they were planning.

"I wish we had our own men with us," Doc muttered fretfully.

"Yeah," Raider agreed. "Nothin' can mess up a good plan like amateurs."

He and Doc were fully armed, each carrying a Winchester .44-.40 in addition to their pistols. They were lying behind rocks on a hillside overlooking the road. And freezing.

"Damn! Think I'm gonna end up settlin' in California," Raider said.

"I've heard worse ideas," Doc replied softly. Then he stiffened. "Look! There they are!"

Actually, he'd heard them more than seen them. But now, bulking blackly against the black of the night, something was moving down the road from the direction of the mill. At about the same time there was the sound of something being moved up at the head of the gully. The wooden screen hiding the tunnel mouth, Raider suspected. And then lights began to show as several men of Hendry's crew carried their lanterns out into the open.

"They're layin' track," Raider said quietly.

Working quickly by the light of their lanterns, the night shift was indeed laying down temporary rails toward the mouth of the gully. Meanwhile, the wagons from the mill were creaking nearer and nearer.

Tabor, who had crawled over to Doc and Raider from his own post a few yards away, hissed, "Let's blast 'em."

"No," Doc protested. "Let the wagons get down into the gully. Let them start loading. They'll be trapped down there."

"Good thinking," Tabor replied.

God save us from hotheads, Doc thought.

The first of the wagons had entered the mouth of the gully, and now ore trucks were rumbling out to meet them. Men wielding shovels were busily transferring the ore. One wagon was loaded, but others were still waiting outside the gully mouth—it was narrow inside—while others were still creaking slowly nearer.

"A lot of wagons," Doc hissed to Raider. "I guess they only make one run."

"Safer. They get it over with quicker."

And then, disaster. One of Tabor's men, trying to get into a more advantageous position, or possibly trying to make himself more comfortable, slipped on the side of the hill. His ridiculous helmet came bouncing and clattering down, the man cursing in pain as his hip made contact with a rock.

"What the hell was that?" a voice shouted from below. Raider recognized it as Hendry's voice.

"There's somebody up above us," someone else answered.

Doc thought it was Harrison. So he was here in person. Good enough, but things were happening fast. There was a mad scramble below.

"Let's get the hell out of here!" somebody shouted.

Then Tabor stood up. "Open fire!" he bellowed. Instantly the hillsides above both flanks of the road erupted in pinpoints of flame.

"Jesus Christ!" someone screamed from the general area of the wagons.

In the light of the lanterns, Raider could see some of Hendry's crew starting back toward the tunnel mouth.

"No! They'll trap us in there," someone called out, and they ran back out into the gully, sheltering behind the ore cars and the wagons. Bullets could be seen kicking up a dust storm all around them, until someone below had sense enough to shoot out the lanterns.

It was very dark after that—everyone's night vision had been affected by the light, both attackers and defenders—and for a while, although the volume of fire was intense, not much harm was done.

The amount of lead coming from behind the ore trucks and wagons suggested that the ore hijackers were as well armed as their attackers. It was, for the moment, a standoff. However, time was against the defenders. They were surrounded on all sides.

Raider called over to Tabor. "Put some men down the

mine," he hissed. "Cover the entrance to that tunnel."

Tabor muttered instructions to his commanders. Another man was sent into town to gather a posse. Meanwhile, the men below, knowing they were trapped, decided to make a break for it. Yelling and shouting, they burst out in a body, raking the flanks of the hills with fire while using as much cover as they could.

At that moment, the Tabor Light Cavalry charged. Doc saw the flash of sabers as the horsemen swept across the road, smashing into the fleeing men. Shrill screams floated up to him. There was a terrible melee below as the horsemen tried to pen in the thieves. Doc was aware of a few vague shadows fading off into the brush.

"Let's get down there," Raider shouted.

By the time they reached the road, it was all over. The ore thieves had thrown down their guns—the ones who were still in condition to do so. Bodies littered the ground, some of them in uniform. It had been a hard fight on both sides.

"Round 'em up," Raider shouted. He grabbed the arm of a wild-eyed cavalryman, whose sword, already red with blood, was raised over his head, ready for a downward cut at the cringing unarmed man clinging to the bridle of the rider's horse. "It's all over, damn it," Raider shouted.

The madness went out of the rider's eyes. He looked stupidly at his bloody sword. Meanwhile, the saner among them were herding the captives together and disarming those in too bad a shape to be able to throw down their own weapons. Raider quickly went from captive to captive, looking into their faces.

"You!" one man snarled at him. "Hendry thought you was a spy."

"Where is he? Where's Hendry?" Raider demanded.

The man looked disgusted. "Run out on us." he snarled. "As soon as the shootin' started. Told us to open up, an' then, under cover of our fire, he lit out . . . along with that fancy dude, Harrison. I pegged a shot or two after 'em, but they got away."

Raider, Doc, and Tabor had a short conference.

"The mill. Maybe they went to the mill," Doc suggested.

"Probably halfway to Mexico by now," Tabor said disgustedly. "No point in goin' there."

But Doc had his own opinions about Harrison. He didn't look like the kind of man who'd go off with nothing but the clothes on his back. "We'll check anyhow," he said. "Can you give us a couple of your horsemen?"

"Sure. Take 'em."

Quickly collecting their own mounts, Doc and Raider headed in the direction of the mill, accompanied by two of Tabor's more level-headed troopers. The ride to the mill was not that long, but the place seemed deserted when they arrived. Everything was blacked out. They cautiously looked into a couple of the buildings, remembering that their quarry was undoubtedly armed, and very, very desperate. But nothing.

"Where the hell could they have gone?" Doc wondered.

"Harrison's got hisself a big house up that draw," one of the troopers volunteered.

"Well, then, let's go."

Long before they got to the house they could see that it was brightly lit. Figures moved behind windows.

"Must be getting money together, or supplies," Doc shouted to Raider.

"We'll hit 'em before they know what's happening," Raider shouted back, and their little attack force galloped straight into the yard. Raider caught a glimpse of Hendry's startled face, peering out a window, and he slammed three rounds from his Winchester in that direction. Hendry yelped and ducked back into the house.

The four of them swung down from their mounts. "Fan out!" Raider shouted. "Someone get around behind the house."

One of the troopers started sprinting toward a corner of the house. Suddenly a gigantic figure loomed out of the shadow of a bush. Klute! Raider realized. And he was carrying a sawed-off double-barreled shotgun. The trooper tried to bring up his rifle, but Klute let him have one barrel. The load of buckshot hammered the trooper backward, lifting him off his feet. And now the barrels were tracking onto Raider.

"You son of a bitch!" Klute screamed, but by then Raider had his rifle to his shoulder, and his first bullet took Klute high in the left shoulder, spoiling his aim. The load of shot tore splinters from the side of the building next to Raider's head.

Klute staggered backward, his hand groping for the pistol tucked into the waistband of his trousers. Raider levered another round into the chamber and fired again. This bullet slammed into the center of Klute's massive chest. Raider could hear the meaty smack of the bullet, hear Klute's grunt of pain, but still he didn't go down. He tried to raise his pistol, but by then Raider had another bullet into him. Klute's pistol discharged at the ground, the bullet ricocheting past Raider, who, levering his rifle rapidly, sent three more bullets into Klute, hammering him backward, Klute's feet backpedaled as he went down. With a shudder, he died. Raider moved forward cautiously, awed by Klute's enormous vitality. He had no intention of turning his back on the big man until he was certain he was finished.

Meanwhile, Doc had gone charging straight into the house. Hendry popped out of a doorway and the two of them exchanged shots until splinters dislodged by Doc's rifle bullets drove Hendry back out of sight. Suddenly, off to one side, he caught sight of Harrison aiming a pistol at him. Doc raised his rifle and pulled the trigger, only to hear a dry click. His rifle was out of ammunition.

Doc went for his .38, realizing at the same moment that Hendry had once again come into view. Doc was caught between two fires, and he knew he was going to be too late with his pistol. Harrison fired. Doc felt a hammer blow against his side. He staggered backward, trying to fire his pistol, with both Harrison and Hendry shooting at him. The only thing that saved his life was the timely intervention of the second cavalryman, who came charging into the room, blazing away with his carbine. Either Hendry or Harrison shot him in the leg; there was so much lead flying around that it was difficult to tell.

The trooper fell, but by now Doc, lying on his wounded side, was firing too, and the sound of Raider's boots could be heard pounding across the veranda. Harrison, cursing, sent one more shot at Doc, the bullet gouging into the floor by his face, peppering him with splinters. Seconds before Raider ran into the room, both Hendry and Harrison had vanished.

"Doc!" Raider shouted as he saw his partner lying in a pool of blood on the floor. The cavalryman was cursing, holding his wounded leg with one hand while he groped for his fallen rifle with the other.

Raider dropped down onto one knee next to Doc, his eyes flickering around the room, looking for the opposition. "You hit bad?" he asked.

"Don't know. It's in the side," Doc muttered between clenched teeth. He felt numb all over; it hadn't started to hurt really badly yet. "Get the hell after them!"

"Too late," Raider hissed, springing to his feet and running to the front door. Doc could hear the pounding of hooves in between the crashing reverberations of the two or three shots Raider got off after the fleeing duo. "Damn it!" Raider called back to Doc. "They took our horses and run off the other two!"

"Wonderful," Doc murmured. "Wonderful. We let the only two who mattered get away."

And then he passed out.

CHAPTER THIRTEEN

When Doc regained consciousness, a doctor was binding up his side. "Ouch!" he yelped.

Raider loomed over him. "Back with us, I see. Been livin' too soft, too long, to let a little scratch like that put you out."

"It certainly doesn't feel little from my side of the fence," Doc said, grimacing as he tried to move his left arm.

"The bullet grazed your ribs, then lodged in the trapezius," the doctor told him. "I took it out, no bones broken, but enough tissue damage so that it's going to hurt like hell for a while and be a little stiff for a few weeks."

"Oh, wonderful," Doc groaned. "And what about Harrison and Hendry?"

"Lit out for the hills," Raider said. "We're goin' after 'em in an hour or two. Just wanted to see what kinda shape you were in."

"Oh, *great* shape. My god, I was clumsy. Missed every damned shot. Still haven't quite got the hang of that double action."

"You sure as hell was scatterin' 'em around the land-scape," Raider admitted. "Well, we gotta get started."

"We? Who's this 'we' you're talking about?"

"McParland's boys got into town about an hour ago. I'm takin' a few of 'em and goin' after our birds."

Doc noticed then that it was full daylight. He must have been out for quite a while. Raider was right. He was getting soft. That had its advantages, of course. He regretted, in a way, not being able to go after Harrison and Hendry, but then again, it was rough going up in those mountains, and it was bound to get very cold, very soon. And also, since he was obviously going to be an invalid for a while, there was the question of finding a nurse. And he just happened to have one in mind. Kitty.

"What the hell are you smilin' about?" Raider asked him.

"Smiling? Oh... nothing," Doc said hastily. "You know, I hate to see you go up there all alone."

"Sure you do, you lyin' son of a bitch," Raider shot back, but with a grin. "I ain't gonna be alone, though. Gonna have a half-dozen men with me, maybe eight. We'll see how it works out. I'll wire the news back here as soon as I've got our boys locked up nice and safe, wherever we catch 'em."

A few more bantering words and Raider left, more re-lieved than he cared to let on. He'd had a bad moment when he'd seen his partner lying on the floor, leaking blood, but the little bastard always seemed to land on his feet. Raider had no doubt he would make the most of his wound, man-aging to live like a king. Tabor had already said the sky was the limit for any man wounded in his service.

Time to get moving. McParland's thirty men had shown up at dawn, off the first train in, but he didn't intend to use all of them. The word from the locals was that Harrison and Hendry, after raiding an outlying mining camp for more supplies, had been seen heading west up one of the high passes into the mountains. It was going to be hard, slogging work going after them; the weather didn't look good, and too many men might be more burden than help.

Leaving Doc looking relatively chipper, Raider corraled

his men, finally deciding on six, led by an old friend from
the agency, Skip O'Neil. The biggest worry as they readied
themselves for the chase was the lowering sky. It looked
bad, the thickening clouds giving off that baleful glare that
so often means snow. Each man was provided with a heavy
sheepskin coat, if he didn't already have one, and fleece-
lined leather gloves. Every one of them carried a rifle and
at least one pistol.

It was one o'clock in the afternoon when they set out,
the seven of them heading up into the pass through which
Harrison and Hendry had fled. There was no problem following them; their trail was clear enough in the soft earth.
They proceeded by twos and threes at first, while the going
was broad and easy, but then the trail began to narrow and
they formed into a single file.

Raider had every hope of catching his quarry. His men
were experienced, hard riders, and their horses were fresh.
From the tracks, Harrison and Hendry didn't seem to be
making very good time. One of their horses appeared to be
partially lame.

They rode until long after dark. This far up the pass there
were not many alternate turnings the fugitives could take,
and these were carefully checked out by torchlight. Always
the tracks continued straight up the pass. Raider called a
halt only when it began snowing. There was no point in
running the horses into the ground, and besides, the snowfall
would cover the tracks.

It was still snowing at dawn. It had been a heavy fall so
far—about a foot of new snow during the night. Another
thousand feet up above them the snow was much deeper;
there had obviously been snow several times at that elevation
over the past few days. That helped in a way. The fugitives
could not have made it up those snow-choked draws.

It stopped snowing about ten o'clock and the sun came
out for a while, reflecting blindingly off the new snowfall.
It was a beautiful world, white and glistening, the snow's
purity broken only by rocky outcroppings and the dark sheen
of the partially covered evergreens. The sun's rays, bouncing off all that white, created a lot of heat. Sheepskin coats

came off and were tied to saddle strings.

"I don't like this," O'Neil said uneasily, looking up at the slopes above. "Never did get too cold last night, and with all that heavy, wet stuff up there..."

He left the rest unsaid, but Raider understood his concern and shared it. Tons and tons of unstable snow lay above the narrow pass they were ascending. He'd be glad when they topped out, but that might not be today. These were the Rockies, the Continental Divide, and higher peaks lay ahead.

"Look!" one of the men called out. "There's their tracks agin'."

About a quarter mile ahead fresh tracks cut into the pristine white of last night's snowfall. It took some hard slogging to get the horses up to that point, but once there it was easy to see from the tracks that Harrison and Hendry had stayed put until the snowfall stopped, which meant they were probably not very far ahead.

"Everybody keep their eyes open," Raider cautioned his troops.

The trail broadened out a little at that point, with smooth slopes rising slowly to the sides for a ways, then suddenly steepening.

Farther forward the trail narrowed again, coming together at a big outcrop of rock about six hundred yards ahead. Raider was uneasy about that outcropping. Their present position was in plain view from it, and they had very little cover near. He thought he saw movement up there, and then he was certain as a puff of whitish smoke blossomed among the rocks. A second later there was a terrific meaty *thonk* next to him and O'Neil's horse screamed and reared up. The horse had hit the ground by the time the reverberating boom of a large-caliber rifle reached them.

"Git the hell back!" Raider bellowed. "They got a Sharps or a Ballard up there."

A couple of the men pulled their rifles free of their scabbards and began firing back at the rocky outcrop, but all of the men were armed with either .44-.40 or .38-.40 Winchester rifles, firing what were essentially pistol rounds.

They could not hope to match the range of the big buffalo gun firing down on them. Raider saw spurts of snow around the crag, but nothing close enough to be encouraging.

Another roaring boom from above, this time a miss, with snow flying up in a huge plume next to O'Neil, who was disentangling himself from his fallen mount. Raider was furiously herding the men back down the trail. The horses were having trouble turning around in the thick soft snow. A third shot from above struck the rifle of one of the men, turning it into instant junk and tearing it from the man's hands. He yelled in pain, his hands numb and bleeding from the terrific blow.

Then they were under some kind of minimum cover, a couple of stunted trees, but at least they could dismount and lead the horses to a safer spot and then try firing back up at the rock outcropping. Three men were sighting their rifles carefully, squeezing off shots in the direction of the hidden rifleman, but it was next to useless. Only a very lucky shot would hit that man.

Then Raider was aware of a soft sound from above, a sibilant hissing whisper of something sliding. Both he and O'Neil looked up at the same moment and saw a cascade of snow drifting down from the higher elevations all along the crest of the slope above.

"Stop shooting!" Raider bellowed to his men. "You're gonna bring a snowslide down on us!"

The men instantly heeded his warning, looking uneasily up at all those tons of snow perched so precariously above them. However, the rifleman above, equally aware of what was happening, began sending his heavy bullets directly into the snowpack. After three shots there was the sound of more sliding, quickly building to a roar interspersed with ominous cracking sounds.

"Avalanche!" Raider called out. "Get back down the trail!"

The men began to run, most of them leading their horses, but the horses stumbled in the soft snow, holding the men back. The roar was terrifyingly loud now and seemed to be coming from all around them. Raider looked up, staring straight into a mass of snow rushing down on him with the speed of an express train. He instinctively threw himself behind an outcropping of stone, pressing himself as flat as possible, and then the world was blotted out by a murky white storm that seemed to go on forever. Even after Raider was covered he could hear the roar reverberating through the loose snow around him. He worked his elbows, trying to create a breathing space, and to his surprise it was easy. It was quiet at last, and, struggling frantically, Raider was relieved when his head broke through into open air.

At first he could see no one else, only tumbled snow and debris. Then O'Neil broke out of a drift, shaking his head dazedly. A horse's broken leg thrust up out of the snow about forty yards away, waving frantically. The slide had been worst toward the middle of the pass, out in the open, but the rocky outcroppings near the edge had broken the full force of the avalanche.

Another man struggled up out of the snow, then fell back, groaning, "Oh, God . . . my leg."

"Come on," Raider shouted to O'Neil. Together they began searching for their men, working near the fallen horses. Three men were badly injured, and only one of the horses was salvageable. The avalanche had snapped off some of the smaller trees above, and, mixed with the snow, the trees had broken limbs and punctured the bellies of horses.

Bullets from above were still kicking up the snow, but now they were moving targets. Raider and O'Neil shot the injured horses, the ones still alive, to put them out of their pain, while the one still in usable condition was quickly led behind a screen of trees, where the wounded men lay groaning and cursing. The shooting stopped suddenly and Raider saw movement from the crag. A man stood up, then scrambled over the rocks and back out of sight.

"I think they're hightailin' it out," O'Neil said.

"No point in hangin' around. They stopped us dead," Raider said bitterly.

"We still got us a horse," O'Neil growled. "I could go on after 'em."

"Naw," Raider replied, pointing to the mass of snow and

trees blocking the trail above them. "No way to get a horse over that mess. We were lucky as hell to have been as far down the trail as we were. Another fifty yards closer and we'd o' been ground to a pulp."

"You mean we ain't goin' after 'em? We're gonna let 'em get away?" O'Neil said, looking angrily at the dead horses and injured men.

"The first thing to think about is gettin' these men back to some help," Raider insisted.

Two of the men had broken legs and another a dislocated shoulder. Raider put the dislocated shoulder back into place, the injured man howling loudly while two others held him down. Legs were splinted. One of the men with a broken leg was to be put on the remaining horse. He could still ride. The man with the injured shoulder was able to walk, while the third injured man, who had a compound fracture of the femur, lay groaning on the snow while two of his companions cut down some saplings to make a litter for him, to be dragged, travois-style, behind the horse.

While all this was going on, Raider found a willow tree still with a little sap in it. He cut some of the smaller branches and bent them into two ovals about two feet long and a foot wide. Then he found an old buckskin jacket in one of the men's saddlebags and cut the leather into strips, which he wove back and forth and lengthwise across the oval willow hoops.

"Snowshoes?" O'Neil asked.

"Yep. Goin' after 'em on foot." He looked up at the sky. "Gonna be more snow. Kinda think they'll be on foot sooner or later too."

"Wait. I'll make some shoes too."

Raider laid a hand on his arm. "Uh-uh. Somebody's gotta get those hurt men back to Leadville. If it snows some more, you're gonna have to break trail for the horse, and maybe even carry the wounded. Besides, it might be better with one man. Harder to spot, and they won't think anyone's after 'em."

O'Neil reluctantly agreed. He was limping pretty badly now himself, and Raider doubted he'd be able to mush through the snow with any speed, snowshoes or not. Raider's horse was dead, but he rummaged through the belongings in his bedroll until he found a pair of heavy, fur-lined mucklucks, and, taking off his boots, he put them on his feet. He would be carrying the bedroll strapped to his back, so all that went into it were his boots and spurs and a few articles of food and spare clothing. He fastened a sling onto his rifle so that he could travel with his hands free. Then, lashing his feet to the jury-rigged snowshoes, he stood up and tested them. They worked fine. Slinging all his gear, he waved to the remains of his little command, then started up the trail, keeping as much to the cover of the trees as possible.

It was hard work climbing over the snowslide. Thank God it hadn't been a bigger one or they'd all be buried deep, either dead or still suffocating to death.

Raider was very cautious as he approached the rocky outcropping from which the hidden rifleman had visited such disaster on his men, but as he expected, he was long gone, leaving behind only a few glittering shell casings. Just as he'd thought: a Sharps, .50-.95 caliber. If any of those monster slugs had hit the men . . .

Harrison and Hendry's tracks stretched away over the saddle of the draw and down into a level, open area, but the men themselves were nowhere in sight. They were both still mounted, and the going was much easier this side of the crest. They'd be gaining on him.

Raider turned around. He was just able to make out the men below. They were fastening the travois litter behind the horse and lashing the man with the badly broken leg onto it. Raider waved and was pretty sure it was O'Neil who waved back. Then he shuffled down over the saddle, skidding his snowshoes along, determined to follow his quarry until he ran them into the ground.

CHAPTER FOURTEEN

Like most horsemen, Raider was not accustomed to walking. Nor did he like it, especially on snowshoes. However, the first day went well enough. Raider was tired when he made camp for the night, but in a good frame of mind. Alone in the vastness of the wilderness he felt very free.

The higher he went into the mountains, the more the scenery was dominated by snow. It was a still, unmoving world of snow-draped pines, huge fields of powdery white crystal, jagged outcrops of rock free of snow where the slope was too great for the white stuff to cling, and a sky so blue it was almost purple, with an occasional cotton-white cloud scudding past high up, sometimes snagging a mountain peak.

Mountains, mountains, and more mountains. When he was high enough for a panoramic view, row upon row of majestic jagged peaks. Geologically it was a new mountain range and still forming. A harsh and unforgiving land. The stupid seldom survived it, nor did those who needed human companionship.

Raider thought of the old mountain men who had roamed

118

through this wilderness two generations earlier, trapping beaver, avoiding Indians, sometimes fighting them because fighting was a sport to the Indians and it was hard to avoid it if they wanted to play. He thought of Jim Bridger, of Jedediah Smith, and of Grizzly Joe, who killed a grizzly bear with a hunting knife at great physical cost to himself. After his companions abandoned him, horribly mutilated, he *crawled*, because his legs were broken and his back shredded, several hunded miles, driven on by a desire for revenge. He even managed to kill a couple of Indians along the way who were intent on killing him. Men like that, strong men, had spent the whole of the winter months alone in these mountains, running their trap lines, hunting, surviving, and finally, after the spring melt, after the winter's solitude and hardships, meeting together at the Rendezvous for an orgy of drinking, gaming, fighting, music, and whatever favors the Indian squaws were willing to grant. Or have taken from them.

By the end of that first day Raider felt the quiet and vastness of the mountains seeping into him. His camp was simple—a small lean-to of pine boughs, with pine needles for a bed. He spread out his bedroll, which consisted of heavy quilted soogans covered by a canvas and oilcloth exterior to keep out the wet, with a flap at the top to cover his head if needed. He'd made the soogans himself out of an old woolen overcoat and cotton batting. Before going to sleep he heated a can of pork and beans over a small, almost smokeless fire, and washed them down his throat with a little coffee. He didn't have much of the coffee and he hoped to make it last.

Then, as the last of the setting sun turned the snow around him to an otherworldly red, he slid into his bedroll and lay quiet for a while, watching the last of the light go from out of the day, turning from rose to blue to purple to black. There was no moon out yet, and when the sun had gone the stars spread from horizon to horizon, a glittering display of distant jewelry, the Milky Way cutting its way through the center, so thick he couldn't see through it. And then he slept.

Breakfast was a bit of bacon and some hardtack. He had pemmican to chew on the trail. He needed food that would create heat and energy, and the concentrated meats, fats, and sugars in the pemmican would help.

It was very difficult to get started that second day. His body ached from the unaccustomed walking, especially his legs and buttocks. The air temperature was near zero, but an hour of walking in the bright sunlight started him sweating, heating and softening his stiff muscles. Even so, he made poor time that day.

His aching muscles were at their stiffest the morning of the third day, but after a half-day's walking he began to feel fine. He felt like he could walk on forever, which was probably true, given the food and rest required to fuel his body. Man, after all, had developed as a walking, running creature, and his amazing muscular legs are easily capable of serving him all his long life, if they are not allowed to atrophy.

Food began to be a problem the third day. He had purposely taken very little with him because of the weight. On the fourth day he shot a rabbit. The big hare had been sitting motionless, expecting its white winter coat to make it invisible against the snow, but Raider saw it and shot its head off with his rifle at a hundred yards. He was so hungry that he gathered twigs right there to start a fire, then quickly skinned and dressed the rabbit. His mouth watered as he cooked the animal. He ate most of it, keeping one of the legs to munch along the trail.

The next day was a hungry one. He went to sleep after eating the last of the pemmican and hardtack. Just a handful. His stomach hurt, but he knew that was often the lot of the hunter.

During all this time he had come across evidence of Harrison and Hendry's passage: tracks in the snow, the blackened ring of a campfire, and, most importantly, the gutted carcass of a deer left hanging from a tree. The meat they had not taken with them was frozen and still good, so Raider cut loose and cooked all he could eat or carry.

They were quite a ways ahead of him. They still had

their horses, although one of the animals was obviously, from the tracks it had left, limping badly. There was an occasional patch of blood in its hoofprints. It had not snowed again since the day they'd started out, so the horses were still useful. However, having the horses meant that the fugitives had to pick their way carefully. Raider, on the other hand, was able to proceed over very rough terrain, cutting miles from his route. There was no need to follow directly on their trail. This high in the mountains there could be no doubt as to where they were heading—Gunnison, on the other side of the continental divide.

Raider crossed the divide on his seventh day. He was by then even leaner and harder than usual. He had sprouted a beard, his sheepskin coat was crusted with snow, and ice kept forming on his mustache and around his mouth as his moist breath froze on contact with the air. He was beginning to look like one of the old mountain men he so admired.

It was growing steadily colder, dropping well below zero at night. Raider was sleeping in all his clothes now inside his bedroll, including the sheepskin coat.

Either cold or hunger did in one of the fugitives' horses. Raider found the carcass of the animal just before he crossed over the divide. Neither Harrison nor Hendry was breaking trail for it. The snow was quite hard within a couple of inches of the crust, so it was possible to walk on it without snowshoes. Raider picked up his pace a bit. They were almost within his reach.

He knew when he was on the continental divide. He had equally spectacular views to both the east and the west. After pausing for an hour to eat and to admire the view, he started out again, moving faster, letting himself half slide down the slippery slopes, fascinated by the smooth response of his leg muscles. He wondered why he had never before liked walking.

But the weather was worsening. The temperature dropped. Clouds began to form. A storm was coming, and the rising wind suggested it was going to be a bad one. The wind intensified the cold, tearing the heat from Raider's body. It began to snow. Soon he had almost no visibility. He tried to keep going, but the cold and the wind and the deepening powder began to exhaust him. A hundred yards felt like ten miles.

The only thing to do was to dig in, seek shelter. Raider began digging a hole in the side of a large snowbank, at first using the butt of his rifle for a shovel. Then, when the snow became harder further down, he took out his bowie knife and cut himself a deep den. He left it large enough inside so he could change his position, then cut snow blocks from the back of the little cave and blocked up the opening.

Now he no longer suffered from the wind, and his body heat raised the temperature of his snow shelter just enough to sustain life. Raider crawled into his bedroll and lay back, conserving his strength, chewing from time to time the last of his cooked deer meat.

The blizzard lasted the rest of that afternoon, the entire night, and a good part of the next morning. Finally, when there was no longer the sound of the wind outside, Raider broke open the entrance to his shelter and peered out. An enormous amount of soft powdery snow had been dumped on the landscape. It was snowshoe time again. Raider was aware, as he started out, that he was beginning to grow weak from lack of food. He would have to move quickly.

For two days he made his way down the west slope of the Rockies, growing more and more gaunt. On the second day he discovered that Harrison and Hendry were both on foot now. He didn't find the remains of the second horse; it had probably been buried by the storm. The men, however, were still carrying on.

They're tough, Raider thought. And able.

The morning of the third day he began to see signs of civilization—a path, an abandoned cabin, cut tree stumps— and he knew he was now not far from Gunnison. He pressed on, hoping to catch up with his quarry before they made it to the railroad and vanished into the general population.

But the weather was not cooperating. The western slope of the Rockies catches the moist air from the Pacific and has a great deal more precipitation than the eastern slope. Another blizzard was brewing. Raider felt the wind rising, and it began to snow in the early afternoon. But still he pressed on. He had no food and was half starved. Besides, he figured he had to come to some kind of settlement soon.

He was passing through rough, partially logged-over country now. Less opportunity to burrow into the snow, nor did he want to. He kept pushing on, realizing he was being foolish, but also knowing how badly he wanted to catch up with Harrison and Hendry.

It was nearly dark when he realized he had gone past the point of no return. The wind and the cold and the clinging snow were killing him. He felt his body going numb, his brain fogging up. He was probably too exhausted by now to make himself a shelter. He staggered on, looking for some kind of natural cover, anything to protect himself from that awful wind. He began to doubt he would make it. Visibility was terrible. Each mass of trees looming out of the murky whiteness of the storm looked for a moment like a building and hope would flair in his heart, but then his refuge would dissolve into more wilderness.

It was almost full dark when he realized he was hallucinating. The blank side of a log cabin loomed ahead of him, but he knew it was only a fall of wind-toppled trees. What really convinced him it was a mirage was the ghostly figure that came toward him, moving soundlessly over the snow, a ghost shrouded in dark baggy clothing. Damned if it didn't look like a skirt with a man's overcoat thrown over it.

And then he was looking into huge blue startled eyes only a couple of feet from his own. As he toppled forward into the snow, the girl dropped the armful of wood she was carrying and ran toward the cabin, crying, "Pa! Pa! Come quick!"

CHAPTER FIFTEEN

Raider felt as if he were floating up out of a deep pit. He was lost, disoriented. As he began regaining consciousness he became aware of intense pain in his feet, as if they were being flayed alive. "Ah!" he cried out, finally coming awake.

The scene that met his eyes was not the scene he expected. He was in a dimly lit, cluttered room, a good-sized room with log walls. A man and a woman were bending over him, looking down quizzically. And still that intense pain in his feet. "What the . . . ?" he burst out, quickly sitting up.

More revelations. He was naked underneath a pile of blankets, and a young girl with long blond hair and huge blue eyes was massaging his feet. Those were the same big blue eyes he'd seen in the face of the ghostly figure approaching him in the storm.

"Just lay yourself back, stranger," the man bending over him said. "Susie's just massagin' your feet. Come near to losin' the damned things from frostbite."

"Feels like I already did," Raider gritted between his teeth as he sank back onto the bedroll.

"Just the feelin' comin' back," the woman by his side said.

Raider took a more careful look around. The cabin he'd seen obviously hadn't been a mirage. Nor the girl. The room itself was quite large, with a potbellied stove near one wall that was putting out wonderful waves of heat. He saw a ladder that probably led up to a sleeping loft. A low narrow door led into another room. The door was partially open, and he could see a narrow cot in the room and a few dresses hanging on pegs. That room had a small stove. In all, a cozy refuge.

Raider was lying on top of his bedroll on the floor, not far from the stove, with a mound of blankets piled on top of him. But he was still cold. It felt as if a terminal chill had soaked clear through to his bones.

"My clothes . . . my gear . . ." he muttered.

"We took your clothes off. They was frozen stiff," the woman replied. "Your rifle and your pistol's over in the corner."

"You . . . took off my clothes?" Raider asked.

"Me an' Susie," the woman said.

Raider glanced down at the girl who was still massaging his feet. He thought he saw her repressing a sly grin, but he couldn't be sure. At least his feet weren't hurting so badly any more; the girl was doing a good job. He was vaguely aware that she was pretty, in a rather unkempt woodsy way. Her mother—he assumed the other two people were her father and mother—had much the same features and the same blue eyes and blond hair, but the wilderness had worn away any prettiness in the older woman. It was one thing to think of the mother undressing him. But Susie . . .

"Name's Slade, stranger," the man said, addressing him. "This here's my wife, Mary Jane, an' my daughter, Susie. Susie's the one who found you wanderin' around out there in the snow, just about a hunnert percent done in. For a while there we wasn't sure you was gonna make it. Cold does funny things to a man."

"I gotta thank you all," Raider replied. "Name's Raider. I was comin' over from Leadville way."

Slade's eyebrows shot up. "A hell of a route you took. It's longer to go around the mountains by train, but you're a hell of a lot more likely to get through, this time of year."

Meanwhile, Mrs. Slade—Mary Jane—had gone to a small cookstove and was putting something that steamed into a bowl. She came back to Raider, carefully keeping the bowl level. "Some soup for you, Mr. Raider," she said in a dried-out but friendly enough voice. "It'll put some heat back in your bones."

Raider skidded up higher on his bedroll, propping his back against the wall. He was careful to keep the blankets from sliding off his lower body. Mary Jane laid the soup bowl on his lap, and Raider tried to start eating it, but he found that his hands were still so cold that he couldn't hold the spoon.

"Here . . . let me do it, mister," Susie said.

She stood up, abandoning his feet, then sat on the edge of his bedroll nearer his head. Picking up the spoon, she began feeding it to Raider, spoonful by spoonful.

"Damn, that tastes wonderful," Raider murmured as the soup trickled into his shrunken stomach.

"That'll sure put some heat back into you," Slade said.

"We oughta open us up a hotel and restaurant out here, Pa," Susie said. "With all these people comin' through."

Raider caught a flicker of annoyance in Slade's eyes. "Oh?" Raider said casually, between spoonfuls of soup. "Somebody else been by?"

Slade hesitated, then said somewhat reluctantly. "Strange enough, Raider, a couple o' other gents came through from your direction yesterday."

"They still around?" Raider asked quickly, glancing over at his rifle and pistol.

"Nope. Sold 'em a couple o' horses an' they took right

off. Said they wanted to beat the storm into Gunnison. Friends o' yours?"

"Not likely. Sure like to catch up to 'em, though."

Slade chewed his cud a moment. "Sounds to me like you're followin' 'em."

Raider wondered if Slade had any connection with Harrison and Hendry, then decided to gamble that he didn't. "There's probably a pretty good reward on their heads right now."

"You a bounty hunter?"

"Uh-uh. I ain't after the reward."

"You the law?"

"Kind of."

Slade chewed that one over, then swore softly. "Damn! Reward, you say, an' I had 'em right here. Coulda stuck a gun in their ribs." Then he grinned. "Don't nohow matter. I charged 'em plenty for the horses."

"You got other horses to sell?" Raider asked.

"That's about all I got. I charge an arm and a leg, though."

"I ain't about to complain, after what you've done for me. Maybe in the mornin' . . ."

"Sure enough . . . if you're feelin' strong enough to ride."

"Let's just figure we got us a deal."

Slade nodded, then went over to a table where his wife had set up three more bowls of soup. "You comin', Susie?" he asked.

"Just as soon as I finish givin' Mr. Raider his soup, Pa," the girl replied.

"I think I can do it now," Raider protested.

"Oh no, I don't mind at all," the girl said. She was leaning quite close, and he was intensely aware of those big blue eyes. She was looking at him in a way he couldn't quite figure out. Something was glittering in those eyes. Humor? Nervousness?

He found out when the soup was finished. The girl laid the bowl down on the floor, but before she got up she looked around quickly. Seeing her parents' hunched over, eating their soup, she grinned wickedly at Raider and, to his amazement, slid her hand under the blankets and gave his cock a squeeze.

Raider let out a surprised garble of sound. The Slades' heads swiveled in his direction, Ma and Pa, but by then the girl had both hands demurely clasped together and was standing next to his bed.

"You all right, Mr. Raider?" Mary Jane Slade asked.

"Ah...just a little twinge in my feet," he mumbled, risking a quick look up at the girl. She was standing facing him, with her back to her parents. She gave him another slow smile, this one just as wicked as the last. Then she went over to the table and sat down and began calmly eating her soup.

After dinner, Slade walked over to the mantel and took down a stone jug, which he brought over to Raider's bedroll. "Since we're gonna be doin' some horse tradin' in the mornin', Raider, this calls for a little social drink," Slade said. "Susie, bring us a couple o' glasses."

"Sure, Pa."

The little social drink turned into a night of heavy boozing, at least for the Slades. Mary Jane joined in right alongside her husband, sitting at the table, nursing glass after glass of what tasted to Raider like bottled panther piss. Raider begged off any heavy drinking on the grounds that he was still weak from his ordeal in the storm. He saw Susie sneaking sly little sips of the whiskey as she brought more for her father, and the more she drank, the more wicked became the covert grins she was sending in Raider's direction.

Finally the stone jug was blessedly empty, and the Slades, mother and father, were barely in condition to make it up the ladder to their sleeping loft. Susie had to stand below, boosting them up. Raider heard a few muttered curses from above, the sound of bodies thumping down onto a bed, then, almost instantly, a duet of drunken snores.

That left Raider alone with the girl. She was bustling about, stacking the dirty glasses in the sink. She seemed to be making no moves toward her room. "Uh...Susie," Raider mumbled.

"You just hold on, Mr. Raider. Ma'll skin me alive in the mornin' if'n I leave these glasses lyin' around."

Not knowing what to expect, but decidedly uneasy nevertheless, Raider watched the girl move busily around the room. Then, smiling at him over her shoulder, she finally went into her own room. But she didn't close the door. Raider watched her light a lantern.

Then she began undressing. She carefully hung her rather shabby dress on a peg. She had long underwear on under the dress; Raider had noticed earlier how rather shapeless the girl looked. But no longer. Under her winter clothing, under all that backwoods poverty, the girl had an amazingly lovely body. Raider watched her pull the tops of her longjohns up over her head, her taut, pink-nippled breasts rising with the movement, too solid to even quiver.

When she'd freed herself from the bottoms of her underwear, Raider found himself staring at a perfect little golden V of soft-looking fuzz, nestled up between long sturdy legs. The girl looked over at him, smiling archly, then turned her back to put away her longjohns. Raider now had a marvelous view of a sleek, heart-shaped little ass.

The girl blew out the lamp in her room and came walking toward him, stark naked, her eyes no longer glittering but smoldering. She was heading straight toward his bedroll.

"For God's sake, your ma and pa," he hissed, glancing nervously up at the ceiling, half-expecting to hear those snores replaced by a bellow of righteous rage.

The girl knelt by his side, her soft little nipples only inches from his face. "Oh, don't worry yourself none about them, Mr. Raider. Ma keeps laudanum in the medicine chest. I put some in their whiskey. They ain't gonna wake up for a long, long time."

And then she was sliding under the blankets with Raider. He felt her velvety skin gliding by his. God, she was hot! Her body seemed to be on fire. His own skin burned where she came into contact with him. He felt the softness of her breasts pressing against his arm. Now he was hot too.

Her hand groped down toward his loins, eagerly, hungrily. "I saw your thing when I undressed you," she said excitedly. "It looked like it was one of 'em that could get real big."

"So I been told," Raider muttered. He gasped as her hot little fingers wrapped themselves around his aforementioned "thing." She began moving her hand wildly. "Oh God, yes," she panted. "Big. And it gets *hard*, too!"

Raider's body was bucking on the bedroll, his hands groping out, running feverishly over the girl's nubile young body. He found her nipples. They were already beginning to swell, but retained that young-girl softness. His right hand slid up the silken inside of one of her thighs, the top edge of his index finger sinking into hotness and wetness. The girl was gushing like a geyser.

Raider tried to roll on top of the girl, but she stopped him. "No," she panted. "Ma says you're still kinda weak. Let me do it all."

She was straddling him then, leaning forward as her right hand guided him into her. It was a hell of a tight fit, but she wasn't going to let that stop her. She rammed her hips down hard, impaling herself on his cock, surrounding it with moist heat. Down and down she pressed, until her buttocks came to rest against his loins.

"Now," she hissed, her eyes glowing hotly, "let's fuck."

By this point, Raider was all for the idea, and seizing her hips in his big hands, he began guiding her pelvis up and down, gasping as he felt her vagina slide against his prick. She moaned, her head thrown back, her lips parted in ecstasy. Then she began moving with an expertise that amazed him, sitting up straight, her full breasts ready for his hands. He reached up, caressing the warm firm mounds, teasing the nipples. Susie moaned again, her hips moving in a wild thrashing circle, driving him crazy.

"Oh God!" she whimpered. "I sure do love this. Love it . . . love it . . . *love* it. Ain't no way to live without it."

They climaxed together in wild, shuddering spasms. Raider watched a slow flush turn the upper part of the girl's breasts a soft, deep red, then mount her neck and climb up into her face. Her eyes glittered hotly, looking unseeingly past him. He felt her inner muscles pulling at him as he unloaded into her, her sleek stomach flexing in the most lovely way.

And then she was collapsing on top of him, panting tiredly but triumphantly, her breasts pressing against his chest. "It's been such a damn long time, mister," she murmured.

"You mean, way up here . . . a young girl like you . . . ?"

She nibbled his ear. "There ain't a hell of a lotta other things to do in this pit. Used to be a family lived about three miles west. They had a son, Jamie. He's the one I done it with first. Now I just have to wait until somebody comes by."

"How old are you?"

"Seventeen."

"Ummmmnnn."

She grinned at him. "You warmer now?"

"Yeah. So warm I can't remember ever bein' cold."

She rolled off him and cuddled up at his side. Together, under the blankets, they formed a private little pool of shared heat. About half an hour later they made love again, this time more slowly, with Raider leading the way.

"Oooohhhhhh," she whimpered softly. "Ain't nobody ever done it to me that way before. It's so *deep!*" A moment later she was swept away on a wave of shuddering ecstasy.

They fell asleep after that, but the girl left his bed sometime during the night while he slept. Raider was awakened in the morning by a terrible groan from above.

"Ooooohhhhhh . . . my fuckin' head!"

"You shouldn't oughta swear like that, John," Mrs. Slade said reprovingly, but it was clear from the tone of her voice that she herself wasn't feeling too good.

Raider slid out of his bedroll and began to pull on his clothes, wanting to be up and dressed before the Slades descended the ladder from the loft. His legs were a little rubbery; he didn't know if that was from his ordeal in the blizzard or from last night's romp with Susie. He was pulling on his shirt when she came out of her room, fully dressed and smiling. She moved right up to him, running a hand through the hair on his chest and grinning.

"Ouch!" he yelped as she gave his crotch a playful squeeze. Then she moved away as her father's legs dangled from the trap door to the loft, his feet searching for the rungs of the ladder.

Breakfast was a glum affair, with the older Slades barely able to eat. Susie bustled about again, doing the cooking and serving, casting humid looks in Raider's direction that he was certain were going to tip off her parents.

But nothing seemed able to get through those monumental hangovers. Raider was even able to swing a fairly good deal on a horse and saddle. Finally, about ten in the morning, he swung aboard. "Got to thank you again," he told the Slades. "All of you."

"It was a pleasure, Raider," Mary Jane Slade said.

"A real pleasure," Susie added. She walked boldly up to his horse and looked him straight in the eye. "You try and come back this way sometime. Hear?"

"I've heard worse ideas," he drawled laconically, nodding at the girl. Then he turned his horse and trotted out of the yard.

CHAPTER SIXTEEN

It was a short run down into Gunnison. Raider took it easy at first; it felt good to be on a horse again, but he was still a little weak from his long cold hungry trek over the continental divide.

Once in Gunnison, he headed straight for the sheriff's office. The sheriff, a burly man with a heavy square face, looked at him doubtfully when he described himself as a Pinkerton man, but his manner perked up when he heard about a possible reward for Harrison and Hendry. After that point, he couldn't help enough. Rewards were a conscious ploy of the Pinkerton National Detective Agency to gain the cooperation of lawmen. Pinkerton agents themselves were not eligible for the rewards. That money was meant to continually sweeten the pot of official and public cooperation in the running down of wanted men.

The sheriff was as disgusted as Slade had been. "Yep. Two men come through here a coupla days ago, lookin' real trail worn. I was onto 'em right off, because I saw they was ridin' a coupla John Slade's horses, but they had a bill of sale, so I let 'em go on through."

"Which way'd they head, sheriff?"

"Took the train down toward Montrose. From there they could either go on up to Grand Junction and points north, or head south for Ouray. If the track is open this time o' year."

Raider thanked the sheriff, then sought out the telegraph office. He was going to telegraph ahead to have the fugitives stopped.

"Sorry, stranger," the telegraph operator told him. "Somebody tore up one hell of a string o' the line between here and Montrose. Gonna be another day before we get it all put back together."

Raider was almost certain it had been Harrison and Hendry who'd taken out the telegraph. All he himself could do was sit fuming, waiting for the next train, while his quarry increased their lead. Finally the train came. Raider arranged to have his horse shipped with him. It was dark, however, before the train came into Montrose.

Here he had a little better luck. The agency maintained a network of paid informers throughout the country. There was one in Montrose, the ticket clerk at the train depot. Raider searched in his memory for the man's code name. He always felt silly using code words, but when he spoke the right one, the ticket clerk eagerly responded.

"Sure," he said in a hushed, conspiratorial whisper. "Two dudes like that came through here a coupla days ago. I thought they was real shifty-lookin' straight off."

The man stopped here in his narrative, looking at Raider meaningfully.

"So? What'd they do?" Raider demanded.

But the informant was not going to have his personal little drama rushed. "I kept a real eye on 'em. They went into town and had 'em somethin' to eat at Maude Kelly's place. It's a restaurant."

"And?" Raider prompted.

"They each had 'em a big steak. A hell of a big steak. An' then they went over to the saloon and put down a few beers."

"And then I suppose they took a leak," Raider said in a dangerously level voice.

The ticket agent looked surprised. "Yeah. They did. How'd you know?"

"Shit, man!" Raider exploded. "Just tell me where the hell they are right now!"

The ticket agent looked offended. "How the hell should I know? They took the next train out to Ouray."

Since there was no other train in that direction leaving earlier than the next morning, Raider had to spend the night in Montrose. But after he had put his horse up at the livery stable, and booked a room for himself above Maude Kelly's restaurant, he sought out the telegraph office. The night man was on duty, and for the next hour Raider kept him busy. First he telegraphed ahead to all stations down the line to alert the local law to be on the lookout for Harrison and Hendry. Then he telegraphed to Leadville, to let Tabor and Doc know he'd made it through the mountains and was still after the fugitives. His last message was to the Denver office, asking McParland to wire extra expense money ahead to Durango, which would be his next major stop.

It was a short train ride the next morning to Ouray. To proceed further by train necessitated going overland, up into the mountains again, to pick up the narrow-gauge line that ran down the gorge of the Animas River, from Silverton to Durango. Finding that his quarry had indeed gone that way, Raider started his horse up the grade, and before long he was once again slogging through deep snow, but this time on a well-delineated road. By the time he got to the railhead, the little train was waiting, ready for its forty-five-mile trip to Durango.

After boarding his horse, Raider climbed up into one of the narrow little cars. "Damned cramped in here," he observed to the conductor.

"Oh, that's because of old man Palmer, you know," the conductor replied. "He was the one started most of the Colorado lines. Had a real strong thing about morality. He figured that wide-gauge trains were a tool o' the devil, because you could get two berths in a cabin. Made his train real narrow, so you could only fit in one berth—and one berth, one person. No chance of old devil sin sneakin' in then. Or so he figured. I could tell him some real interestin' stories, though, o' the kinda things that go on in them straight and narrow berths o' his. Seems there's no stoppin' some people when they get a certain idea stuck in their mind."

Remembering Susie, Raider had to agree. Then the train was off. Raider sank down into a seat, and although he was chafing at the bit, thinking of all the distance Harrison and Hendry had gained on him, he could not help but admire the view from the train window. The surrounding scenery was stupendous. For almost the whole way the train ran along a huge gorge cutting through rugged mountain scenery.

When he got to Durango, Raider found several messages waiting for him at the telegraph office. Among others, McParland had wired him the money he'd asked for, along with a demand for a strict accounting of any expenditure over fifty dollars, as per company regulations.

Once again, Raider sought out the local law, and discovered that two men fitting the descriptions of his boys had left the railroad here at Durango and were last seen heading due south, into New Mexico. Raider had little choice except to follow.

"Don't know as how I'd like to be goin' down that way myself," the sheriff told him. "The Utes are actin' up again. They got 'em a big reservation down there just below the Mesa Verde area. Ain't many white folks down that way. You'll be more or less on your own."

As Raider was digesting this cheerful information, he noticed a stack of wanted posters sitting on the sheriff's desk, still bound up with twine. On a hunch he asked the sheriff to open them up.

"They just come in on the train this mornin'," the sheriff informed him.

Sure enough, there they were at last, the flyers on Harrison and Hendry, printed on the standard Pinkerton National Detective Agency form. The agency name was emblazoned across the top in an undulating curve, decorated with little leaves. Under the name was a single open eye, with the logo beneath it, "We Never Sleep." The addresses of the company offices were listed below: Chicago, Philadelphia, New York, Boston, St. Paul, and Denver. The agency was offering five hundred dollars reward apiece for each of the culprits, with Tabor offering a further five hundred. A thousand dollars in all for each man—a princely sum, and one certain to arouse the greed of every bounty hunter in the West.

The descriptions of Harrison and Hendry followed, with the warning that they were undoubtedly armed and could shoot like hell. Raider asked the sheriff for a few of the wanted notices, which he stuffed into his coat pocket. After thanking the sheriff, he bought provisions for a week. Then, mounting his horse, he headed south, into the high, dry country of the Four Corners area, where Colorado, New Mexico, Utah, and Arizona come together. Empty, dangerous country, where, by himself, he was going to have to bring two dangerous men to bay.

CHAPTER SEVENTEEN

The terrain was changing considerably. Raider had left behind the heavily wooded, steep mountain country and was now entering a region of high plateaus. The weather was much warmer and drier, with the daytime temperature well above freezing. The ground was clean and dry and for the most part level.

As he went farther south, the landscape became dominated by high flat buttes, colored a variety of pastels and ochers. Raider liked this country. He liked its openness, the immense vistas. He never tired of the incredible variety of scenery the West had to offer. Once more on a horse, he forgot for the time being why he was here.

He abruptly remembered later that afternoon when he saw a distant figure come into view from the mouth of a canyon, moving in his direction. Raider immediately guided his horse behind the cover of a small outcropping of sandstone. Dismounting, he took his field glasses from his saddlebags. Resting his arms on the sandstone, he studied the distant figure. It appeared to be an Indian, loping steadily along on foot at a slow run.

As the Indian grew closer, Raider saw that it was an old man. He would never have guessed it from the way the old fellow was steaming along. But then, the Indian appeared by his dress to be from one of the Pueblo tribes, and they had a reputation as runners.

When the old man was only a short way off, Raider mounted and rode his horse out into the open, heading for the Indian. The Indian looked up, startled. He came to an immediate stop, studying Raider, looking for a moment as if he were thinking of taking off in another direction, but then he seemed to realize that it would probably be a waste of time to run away from a mounted man.

The old Indian stood waiting motionless as Raider rode up to him.

"Hello, Grandfather," Raider said as he reined in his horse about ten yards from the man.

The Indian made no response, simply looked up at Raider, his face expressionless.

Raider dismounted, and, to show he meant no harm, he squatted on his haunches near the Indian, putting himself lower than the other man. "Where do you come from?" Raider asked.

The old man showed no comprehension of Raider's words, but now he too hunkered down; he and Raider were now separated by only a few yards. Raider searched in his mind for some appropriate words in an Indian dialect, but could not string enough together. Besides, the Indian probably spoke a different language anyhow. Doc had once told him that there were hundreds of Indian languages.

Finally, he got the bright idea of trying Spanish, which proved rewarding. *"Buenas tardes. Dondé va?"*

The old man's face showed a flicker of comprehension, but those obsidian eyes were not about to give anything away. *"Buenas tardes, señor,"* he replied in a strangely accented Spanish, then continued in the same language, "I go to my cornfield. To care for the plants."

"Do your people live near here?"

The old man pointed back the way he had come. "Two hours' run in that direction," he said vaguely.

Raider looked doubtful. He'd seen the way the old man had been flying along. Two hours of it? He looked as if he had to be at least in his seventies. Raider shrugged. "I am looking for two white men," he said. "Perhaps you or some of your people might have seen them."

The old man looked very interested now, but still he hesitated. Raider decided to gamble. "They are bad men. I have come to take them back to the white man's justice."

A flicker in the old man's eyes was the closest he came to genuine excitement. "It is as you say," he replied quietly. "They are bad men."

"You know where they are, then?" Raider asked, not bothering to hide his own excitement.

The old man nodded. "They are at the place of the Anasazi. And there are more than two now. There are many."

"The Anasazi?" Raider said, puzzled, trying to remember where he had heard that word.

"The Old Ones, señor. They are living in the House of the Old Ones. That is not good."

Then Raider remembered. Anasazi was what the present-day Pueblo peoples called the long-vanished race that had built the huge cliff dwellings in some long-ago time. "Tell me more," he asked the old Indian.

It turned out that two men—and from their description they sounded like Harrison and Hendry—had come through this way a few days before. They had ridden straight to one of the Anasazi's abandoned cliff dwellings, one particularly revered by the local Indians as a holy place. Things such as this had happened before. Fascinated white men had come to look at the impressive ruins, but they had usually gone away again after a day or two. However, these two had stayed, and a day later, several other white men had joined them.

The Indians were in a quandary. They did not like these strangers living on what to them was sacred ground, but neither did they want to cause trouble. The Pueblo were a peaceful people, and they knew that using force against even a few white men might bring down on them the whole weight of the white world. At last they sent a delegation of elders to ask the interlopers to leave. That had been only the day before. The white men had treated these emissaries in a most disrespectful manner, bodily throwing them out, threatening harm to them and to their village if they returned. Even now the tribal elders were trying to decide what to do next.

After the old man had finished, Raider sat in thought. So, Harrison and Hendry had been reinforced by more men. Why? And why here? Why hadn't they kept on moving? Those were questions he'd like to find the answers to. "Can you show me this place?" he asked the old man.

The old Indian sat silently for a while, perhaps reluctant to involve more white men in this tribal difficulty. Finally he stirred himself and spoke. "You wish to take these bad ones away?" he asked.

"I wish to take them to a place where they will no longer be able to bother you."

The old man abruptly stood up. It was an effortless move; he simply seemed to sprout from the ground. Raider enviously hoped he'd be able to move like that when he was as old, but he wasn't hanging too much hope on it.

"I will show you," the Indian said. "But first I must care for my corn."

Raider agreed, even offered to ride the old man double behind him, but the old man politely refused. He started running again at an easy lope. Raider had to put his horse into a trot to keep up with him. It was only a short while later that they reached a stand of corn tucked away in a small ravine that had a trickle of water running through it from a spring higher up. The bright green of the cornstalks was shocking in this muted arid land. The old man picked up a hoe and began weeding, then he scooped water from the tiny stream in a gourd and poured it into the channels running bewteen his rows of corn. Raider noticed that each corn hill had also been planted with beans and squash, forming the staple triad of the ancient Indian way of farming.

The whole process took about an hour, with Raider finally helping with the watering, much to the old Indian's enjoyment. Then the hoe and the gourds were put away and the old man started off at a trot again, Raider riding along beside him. This went on for almost two hours, the old man moving along apparently tirelessly. Raider had heard about this kind of thing but still found it hard to believe. Of course, the old man had undoubtedly been doing it all his life. Still . . .

They had gone about twenty miles when the old man suddenly stopped. "We are close," he said to Raider. He asked Raider to leave his horse and continue on foot. Hesitantly Raider agreed. This was not the kind of country in which he cared to be on foot, nor did his pointed-toed, high-heeled boots help. They were definitely not made for walking.

Fortunately, he only had to walk a few hundred yards. Then, peering from behind a ridge, he found himself looking across a canyon at one of the old cities of the Anasazi.

It was quite large, a complex of buildings and apartments that reminded him of a squared-off beehive, consisting of piled-up rectangular structures made of adobe bricks, perched well back in an immense cut in the side of a towering butte. The cut was natural, but obviously enlarged by the builders, forming a large habitable area under the overhang of the butte. There was no apparent way down to it; the only entrance to the living area was from below, a narrow winding path that became steeper and steeper as it climbed higher, finally ending in a ladder that covered the last twenty yards.

At first Raider thought the complex was deserted, but then he saw the figure of a man lounging on the ground in front of one of the buildings. He had his field glasses with him and brought them up to his eyes. The man sprang into close view. A white man, and a hardcase if Raider had ever seen one.

Then another man came out of a doorway. Bonanza. It was Hendry. Raider noticed a couple of other men standing on the roof of one of the higher buildings. Both men carried rifles. Guards.

Hendry turned and called back through the doorway.

Raider couldn't hear the words at this distance, but he saw Harrison came out into the open. He and Hendry walked across the bare dirt area in front of the building and approached a low swelling in the middle of the clear space. A flat rock lay at the apex of this convex area. He saw Harrison and Hendry struggle with the rock, sliding it out of the way. From where he was watching, which was more or less at the level of the flat area, Raider could not see what lay beneath the stone, but he decided it had to be a hole, because Harrison abruptly disappeared from view. Hendry knelt down by the opening, looking down after Harrison for a while. After about five minutes, Harrison reappeared, climbing up out of the ground. The two men stood there for a few minutes, pointing down into the hole and talking animatedly. Then they pushed the stone back into place and headed back into the shade of the buildings.

Raider scanned the entire cliff dwelling again. Now only the two guards were visible. "What is that hole in the ground?" he asked the old man.

The old man hesitated, then said, "It is a kiva, a holy place. It is where the men go down to dance and to smoke and to talk to the gods and to the Old Ones. Those white men go down into it, and that is not good."

Raider backed away from his vantage point. "Come on," he said. "Let's go meet your elders."

It was less than a half hour to the village, a small collection of low adobe buildings backed up against a cliff. A small spring bubbled clean water out of the base of the cliff. When it was seen that the old man had a white man with him, a crowd quickly gathered, forming a big circle around Raider's horse. The old man pushed through the throng alone, heading for a small group of equally aged men. The village elders, Raider suspected, from the obvious respect with which the other people treated them.

Raider's guide talked animatedly with the elders for a while. All of them kept glancing over at Raider. Finally, he was asked to dismount and approach them. The crowd parted; Raider was beginning to wonder if he'd done the right thing in coming here. There were a hell of a lot of

Indians around him, and he knew they sure as hell didn't have any reason to like white men.

The old men, however, treated him with courtesy. Their friendliness increased when he reaffirmed that he was here to remove the invaders who were desecrating their holy places.

"Do you have someone," he asked, "who can take a message from me to Durango?"

A young man was found. "Our best runner," Raider was told, which probably meant he was pretty damned good. Raider wrote out a message to the Durango sheriff, including the text of a telegram to McParland, asking him to send reinforcements. Raider made certain to give the messenger money, since he would have to wait for the reinforcements to arrive, then lead them back to the village.

It was now growing dark. Raider watched the young man lope off into the night. Food was prepared, and Raider ate with the elders: cornmeal tortillas, vegetables, and a little deer meat. As he ate, Raider was thinking, planning what he would do when the reinforcements arrived. But still those same questions: What the hell were Harrison and Hendry doing holed up in a dead-end trap like that cliff dwelling? Why weren't they still hightailing it, heading for someplace where they would no longer be in danger, such as Mexico, or South America? With all the money they'd got out of Tabor's mine . . .

More importantly, how the hell was he going to dig them out of the cliff dwelling? While a trap for his quarry, it was also a natural fortress. He finally asked his hosts if there was any way into the place other than up the path and the ladder.

The men around him hesitated, which told him there *was* probably another way in, but that it was probably a closely guarded secret. However, necessity convinced the Indians to tell him. Yes, there was another way in, but a very difficult one, along the face of the cliff, passable by only one man at a time.

"I would like to see it now," Raider said.

"In the nighttime? But it would be dangerous."

"I would like to know something about this place of the Anasazi before my men arrive," Raider insisted. "Perhaps lives will be saved."

This made sense to the Indians. Two young men were sent to guide him. First they gave him Indian moccasins to wear, because the route was going to be tricky and his boots would be more hazard than help. However, he did ride his horse as close to the cliff dwellings as he dared before dismounting and putting on the moccasins.

This alternate entrance to the mesa turned out to be a narrow fissure running along the face of the cliff on a level with the cliff dwelling. Nowhere was it more than a foot wide. The only way to traverse it was by utilizing handholds in the soft crumbly sandstone of the cliff face. Fortunately, the cliff face sloped backward at this point, and not out, so while the passage was hair-raising, Raider found it manageable. He doubted, however, if he would have been able to make it without his guides. At points the fissure petered out, and his feet had to be guided into crevices obviously hollowed out by hand.

Finally they were at the edge of the large hollow in the cliff face that housed the cliff dwelling. The Indian guides showed no indication of wanting to go further, and Raider recognized the wisdom of their viewpoint. He now knew a way to get a few men into the level area, enough to pin down Harrison and his men while Raider's reinforcements stormed the path. The smart thing to do now was to go back while he was in one piece. But he felt a strong inclination to satisfy his curiosity. What the hell had Harrison and Hendry been doing inside the kiva?

It lay not far from where he now crouched at the edge of the cliff face. The moon, which had made it easier for him to negotiate his way along the cliff, was far enough down so that the natural overhang of the butte kept its light from illuminating the area of the cliff dwelling and of the kiva. There wasn't a light showing in any of the houses; Harrison's men must be sleeping. True, he thought he could make out the shadowy figures of guards on top of two of the highest buildings, but their view was out over the land

below the butte; the buildings themselves were in the way
of their view of the kiva area.

Damn! Why not give it a try? Signaling his guides to
wait, Raider slowly slipped out into the open, hugging the
shadows. He made it to the flat rock that covered the entrance to the kiva and flattened himself out on the ground
beside it, listening. Nothing. Not a sound. So far he was
undiscovered.

Moving the rock aside was another matter. It was heavy
as hell. He couldn't keep it from scraping as he slid it to
one side. But still no sign of life from the buildings.

Feeling down into the dark maw of the opening with his
hands, Raider discovered that there was a ladder. He quickly
swung his legs down into the opening, hoping to hell there
were no snakes inside. But then, Harrison had gone down
earlier with no signs of trouble.

Before he got to the bottom of the ladder, Raider's feet
came into contact with something hard and with a regular
geometric shape. He squeezed past, but found he could not
go down much farther. Deciding to take a chance, he hung
onto the ladder with one hand while he fumbled in his shirt
pocket with the other, looking for a match. Finding one,
he struck it into life with his thumbnail. The resulting flare
of light blinded him for a moment, but then his eyes quickly
adjusted and he had a moment to look around him before
the match got short enough to burn his fingers.

Goddamn! The kiva was stacked half full with bars of
silver!

So this is what Harrison and company had done with
their loot. Hell, there was a fortune here. Before the match
had gone out, Raider had had a chance to look around pretty
thoroughly. The interior of the kiva was quite large, a big
rounded room, and a hell of a lot of it was filled with silver
bars. No wonder Harrison and Hendry had come here. They
were reclaiming their take from Tabor's mine.

Raider slipped one of the bars into his pocket, then quickly
climbed the ladder and emerged into the open. He started
to slide the stone back into place over the opening to the
kiva but decided against it. Let Harrison and Hendry dis-

cover someone had been inside. Since the cliff dwelling was so difficult to get into, they might think it had been one of their own men. Maybe they'd start fighting one another.

He was about to turn and head back toward the cliff when he heard a sound from a few yards away—the sound of a rock being crunched under a boot heel. He started to spin in that direction, his hand dropping down toward his gun butt, when the light of a bull's-eye lantern suddenly glared into his eyes, blinding him.

"You just go ahead and try for that gun, old hoss," Hendry's voice came out of the dark, quite but deadly. "An' it'll be the last move you ever make."

CHAPTER EIGHTEEN

For the hundredth time, Raider tested the ropes binding him. For the hundredth time, they held. He had to hand it to Hendry—he sure could tie a knot.

He'd let them disarm him when they'd caught him outside the kiva. What choice did he have? The lantern was shining straight into his eyes. There was no way to tell how many men had the drop on him. God, he'd been stupid. The only good thing was that they had no idea that there were two Indians still clinging to the cliff face. Raider wanted to make sure they got away clean.

Hendry wanted to shoot him out of hand, but Harrison had other ideas. "He might be useful to us," he insisted. "We can always shoot him later."

Raider was knocked around for a while. They wanted to know if he'd been alone. "Why waste the time?" Harrison said. "We'll find out soon enough."

"Gimme an hour alone with him," Hendry said, glaring at Raider. "I'll make this fuckin' spy sing like a bird."

That was a theory Raider didn't care to put to the test.

Undoubtedly Hendry would enjoy breaking him. There was no mistaking the hate in his eyes. Fortunately for Raider, there was a diversion. Harrison's head suddenly jerked erect. "What's that sound?" he hissed.

Everyone fell silent, and then they could all hear it—the distant squeal of axles, the braying of a mule.

"It's the wagons! They're here!" Harrison shouted. "Come on!"

Hendry hesitated, his big fist cocked in front of Raider's face. "Come on, I said," Harrison snapped. "We'll need every man."

Hendry snarled something but contented himself with tying Raider up, grinning as he pulled the ropes brutally tight. "I'll have time for you later, spy," he promised.

It was growing light by the time the wagons arrived. There were four of them, each pulled by six mules and driven by one man. Raider, tied to a post about ten yards from the kiva, watched the men laboriously haul the silver up from below, then lower it down the cliff face and load it into the wagons. There was so much silver that it was impossible to load it all. "We'll have to come back someday," Harrison said.

"Hell, we'll be so rich we won't care," Hendry replied, grinning.

"Rich to one man may not be rich to another," Harrison said stiffly.

"Oh, yeah," Hendry sneered. "I keep forgettin' what a big man I'm talkin' to. It's champagne an' caviar for you or nothin', right? Well, for me, I'll take beer and beef, as long as there's plenty of it. All I know is that I ain't never gonna have to work for a livin' again, an' neither is anybody else here. Am I right, boys?"

There was a general murmur of agreement. However, Raider noticed some of the men eyeing the huge load of silver greedily. These were not men from Hendry's original crew. After the shoot-out behind the mine, they were all either dead or in jail. The men now loading the silver were men Hendry and Harrison had had to recruit. They were a hard-looking bunch. Counting the drivers, there were ten of them. Harrison and Hendry were going to have to watch their backs.

They were still loading the silver after dark. The work wasn't finished until after midnight. The men were exhausted, but Harrison demanded that they leave immediately. "We've got to make tracks out of this place," he insisted. "We've been holed up here too long." He pointed to Raider. "He may have help on the way, and if he could find us, so could somebody else."

Grumbling, the men hitched up the mules, and by one o'clock they were ready to leave. Raider was tossed into one of the wagons and lashed to a crossbar. He tried to find a comfortable position, but it was difficult. His hands had long ago become numb, but he'd managed to loosen the ropes around his wrists a little, and now a little bit of feeling was slowly trickling back.

"You'll never make it," he told Harrison, trying to keep his hands out of sight. "The silver's too damned heavy."

"We'll make it," Harrison insisted.

"Yeah . . . all the way to Mexico," Hendry added. "We got the whole thing fixed up with a Mexican bank."

"Shut up, Hendry. You talk too much," Harrison snapped.

"Don't tell me to shut up," Hendry snarled back.

The two men glared at one another for several seconds, until one of the other men said thoughtfully, "So . . . we're on our way to Mexico. That's one hell of a long way, Harrison. Maybe we all deserve a bigger cut . . . if the Mexicans don't take the whole shootin' match away from us."

"Yeah," Raider said. "Those Mexican *federales*—"

"Shut up!" Harrison snarled. Then he turned to the men, all of whom were listening intently. "I'll make sure everyone gets a fair cut," he said. "Now let's get moving."

Whips cracked, mules complained, but the wagons lurched into movement, their broad iron tires crunching loudly over the dry ground. The jolting knocked Raider off balance, but he managed to sit up again. He was glad to be still alive and in more or less good condition. It was a damned lucky thing that Harrison thought he might be more useful alive. But in what way? As a hostage? Maybe he better keep his mouth shut for the time being.

It was a quick dawn, a desert dawn, the eastern horizon brightening swiftly. Then the sun came up from behind a large butte, its rays streaking redly over the awakening landscape, driving away the night's chill. All it took was one touch of that southwestern sun. And as the day grew, the wagons creaked on relentlessly, slow mile after slow mile, leaving their mark behind them. Raider glanced back at the wheel tracks, so clearly etched in the sandy soil. Easy for McParland's men to follow. *If* they were coming. *If* the message had gotten through.

The men were edgy and tired, but they rode a tight guard around the slow-moving wagons. Undoubtedly they too were thinking about the possibilities of being followed.

Around ten o'clock Hendry rode up alongside Harrison, whose horse was plodding along next to the wagon Raider was riding in. "Don't look," Hendry said in a low voice, "but I think I saw somethin' move out in the brush."

"You're sure?"

"Uh-uh. But I'm gonna *make* sure."

Hendry drifted back to the next wagon. Raider could hear him quietly ordering two of the men to circle back about a hundred yards, behind and to the right, and then come riding in hard. The men nodded, their eyes flickering left and right. Raider watched them drift back until they were about a hundred yards behind the last wagon. Then they suddenly whipped up their horses and cut to the right in a big circle, pounding through the brush. Nothing happened for a moment, and then there definitely was movement in the brush. A second later a lone horseman went racing out into the open, heading away from the two men behind him. Raider had a moment to see that it was an Indian, a young brave.

Harrison also had a moment to realize the same, and then he was shouting at Hendry, "No! Don't!"

But Hendry already had his rifle to his shoulder, and he fired. Raider saw the bullet knock a puff of dust from the Indian's buckskin jacket. He reeled sideways, nearly falling from his horse, but with great effort righted himself. Bend-

ing low over his horse's mane, blood darkening the left side
of his jacket, he raced away. Hendry tried another shot
without appreciable effect, and then the Indian was out of
range. The two men behind tried to follow, but the Indian's
pony, much more lightly laden than their horses, pulled
away easily. The men reigned in, looking around them
uneasily, as if expecting more Indians to materialize out of
the brush. They quickly cantered back to the wagons.

Harrison rode up to Hendry, his face dark with anger.
"You idiot!" he shouted. "What the hell did you think you
were doing?"

"Shootin' me an Indian," Hendry shouted back. "What
the hell's wrong with that? I been shootin' Indians all my
life. An' if you call me an idiot ag'in . . ."

"I'll tell you why you're an idiot," Harrison said in a
tight voice. "Because this is *their* country, and there are
only a dozen of us, and we're tied to the speed these wagons
can make. If that Indian makes it back to his village . . . Hell,
if you're going to shoot Indians, make sure you *kill* them."

Hendry blanched a little. "Maybe you got a point," he
admitted. "Ah, what the hell. These damned Pueblo Indians
ain't the fightin' kind. Remember the way we run 'em off
back at the cliff dwellin'?"

"That wasn't a Pueblo Indian," Raider cut in. "That was
a Ute. And *they* are fightin' Indians."

"You're sure about that?" Harrison demanded. "It was
a Ute?"

"Yep," Raider replied laconically.

Harrison looked coldly at Hendry. "Damn you," he said
softly. Then he called out to the men, "Keep the wagons
as close together as you can. Riders, fan out to the sides a
little. You, Jake. Take point."

The men rather nervously took up tighter defensive positions. They were a hard-bitten group, but the fighting
power of the Utes was fresh in everyone's mind. They all
remembered the Meeker Massacre. It had happened only a
little more than three years before. Nathan Meeker had been
the Indian agent at the White River Indian Agency in eastern
Colorado. Meeker had also been a businessman and a stick-

ler for order and Christian morals, as long as they made him a buck. He made the mistake of closing down the track where the Utes exercised their passion for horse racing. The Utes, a fierce and independent people, rebelled; they killed Meeker, nine of his employees, and a dozen cavalrymen sent to restore order. It took the Army a year to pacify the tribe. Now they were supposed to be confined to their reservation. The trouble was, Harrison's little wagon train was right in the middle of the new Ute reservation.

The wagons plodded on, the men growing more nervous as they grew more tired.

"We're gonna have to rest the men and the mules sometime," Hendry complained.

"Tonight," Harrison replied curtly. "We'll find a spot that's easy to defend, then move on in the morning. Let's just hope that Indian fell off his horse and died."

The shadows were growing long when Harrison spotted the place where he wanted to make camp for the night. Raider had to admit he had a pretty good eye for terrain. It lay about a mile ahead, a low round hill rising a little above the surrounding area. It was devoid of brush, and so was the land for a hundred yards around it. With the wagons formed up in a circle, Harrison's men would have a clear field of fire over a full 360 degrees.

"I hear they took away the Utes' guns," Harrison said.

"I heard the same," Hendry replied. "That gives us an edge."

Raider knew that was true. The Utes had been thoroughly disarmed by the Army before being sent into the new reservation. Of course, guns would begin to reappear among them soon enough. There were always white men eager to make a dollar, and there was really no way to avoid it anyhow. After so much contact with the white man, the Indians had become more or less dependent on firearms.

Harrison's entire party received a practical demonstration of the situation a few minutes later. The wagons had drawn a little closer to the hilltop. Harrison turned to one of the men. "Jake," he said. "You ride on ahead and scout that place out for us."

"Ah, shit! Why always me?" Jake groused, but he spurred his horse into a fast trot toward the hilltop. He had only gone about fifty yards when Raider saw something flash in the air, heading for Jake. There was a meaty *thunk,* then Jake cried out and jerked erect in his stirrups. His horse panicked, spinning around to head back toward the wagons.

As Jake slowly fell from his saddle, everyone could see the arrow protruding from his chest.

CHAPTER NINETEEN

Harrison reacted instantly. "Whip up the mules," he shouted. "We've got to beat them to the hilltop!"

Whips cracked. The mules leaned into their traces, jerking the wagons forward. The men began firing into the brush, not so much hoping to hit anything, but simply to keep the Indians out of arrow range. Nevertheless, an arrow thudded into the wood of the wagon in which Raider was riding, very close to his head. He caught glimpses of shadowy figures flitting through the brush.

"It's no good," Hendry bellowed. "They'll be on us before we make it out into the open."

"Then we'll have to give them a diversion," Harrison snarled. He rode his horse close to Raider's wagon, pulling out his sheath knife as he did so. Raider tried to pull away, not wanting his throat cut, but he was tied too tightly to the crossbar. To his amazement, Harrison began cutting him free. His hands were freed last, and he automatically flexed his fingers, glad to see that they worked. It was a good thing he'd been able to loosen the ropes earlier.

155

And then Harrison had him by the arm. Guiding his horse to the side, he jerked Raider out of the wagon. Raider had not expected this, and he was unable to keep himself from falling. Fortunately the wagon was not yet going that fast, and he managed to roll when he hit the ground, breaking his fall. Still, he had the wind knocked out of him. He rolled to a sitting position, staring stupidly up at Harrison and Hendry, who had pulled up their horses nearby.

"What the hell'd you do that for?" Hendry protested. "You ain't lettin' him go?"

"In a manner of speaking," Harrison replied with a slight smile. "I told you he might come in more handy alive than dead. By the time the Utes get through playing with him, we'll be halfway to the hilltop."

"Damned good thinking," Hendry said, guffawing. And then both men wheeled their horses and galloped after the fleeing wagons.

It suddenly occurred to Raider that he was in a very bad position. He quickly got to his feet, staggering a little, stiff after all those hours spent sitting in the wagon. He looked about for a place to hide, but it was too late. A horse broke out of the brush about forty yards away, with an Indian on its back. Horse and Indian were heading straight for Raider, and the Indian was whooping wildly, waving a long, iron-tipped lance. Raider watched the lance come up for the thrust. The Indian was leaning toward him, his face intent beneath the war paint.

Adrenaline pumped through Raider's body, charging his tired muscles. He forced himself not to run, but to hold his ground, watching the sharp iron tip of the lance line up on his chest. The Indian was certain he had him. He squeezed his pony's ribs tightly with his knees, thrusting with the lance, all his efforts concentrated on Raider, who waited until the last moment, until the lance tip was almost touching his chest and the Indian's whole body was committed, until there was no chance of the man changing his aim, and then Raider turned a quarter turn to the side. The lance tip passed so close it ripped his shirt. Reaching up, he seized the shaft of the lance in both hands, then twisted, lifting the Indian off his horse using the leverage of the lance.

The look on the Indian's face would have been comical under other conditions, a look of intense astonishment. He flew through the air and lit on his back, expelling a huge *whoosh* of air. However, he was young and tough and managed to vault to his feet before Raider could reach him. Snarling with a mixture of rage and fear, the Indian drew a long knife and held it out in front of him, facing Raider.

Now Raider had the advantage because of the longer reach of the lance. The two men circled for a few seconds. Then the Indian feinted inward, trying to get Raider to commit himself with the lance. Raider held back until he figured he had the Indian cornered, then lunged forward, aiming the lance tip at the Indian's belly. But his toe caught on a root, and he lurched off balance, the lance tip jabbing the air harmlessly to one side of the crouching warrior.

Now the Indian had the advantage. Slipping inside the area covered by the lance, he grabbed the shaft with one hand and slashed at Raider with the knife. But Raider had by now caught his balance, and, ripping the lance shaft from the Indian's hand, he swung the butt around, catching the Indian alongside the head. The Indian went down, but the lance shaft, already weakened when Raider had unhorsed the Indian with it, broke in two not far from the head. Fumbling wildly, Raider managed to grasp the little bit of shaft still clinging to the lance head. Now all he had was a clumsy knife, not much longer than the Indian's.

Once again the two men began circling one another. They were both panting, both a little tired. Runnels of sweat streaked the dust that coated the Indian's nearly naked body. Raider's shirt was hot and wet and stuck to his back. He still had a chance of coming through this alive, or so he thought until two other Indians, both carrying war lances, rode into view.

One looked like a chief; at least he was wearing the feather warbonnet of a chief. He sat his horse regally, the lance head pointed up at the sky while he perused Raider. Genuinely a noble picture, but Raider had no time to admire the man because he still had the knife-armed Indian in front of him. And now the second mounted Indian, the one next to the chief, was raising his lance and urging his horse forward, and Raider knew that even if he got away from that one, the Indian with the knife would probably kill him.

Then to his amazement, and to the amazement of the other two Indians, the chief suddenly shouted out a command. The Indian on horseback, the one with the upraised lance, hesitated, glancing back at his chief, obviously wanting to get on with the fun and games of spitting Raider like a wild pig, but the chief shouted again and the man reluctantly veered off to the side, contenting himself with tapping Raider on the shoulder with the butt of the lance, counting coup.

Raider continued to stand in a crouch, turning quickly in a complete circle, checking to see that no one was creeping up on him. There were plenty of other Indians emerging from the brush now, all of them armed and mounted and all of them glaring at him with considerable hostility, but not one of them was making a move to attack.

The chief urged his horse forward a few steps in Raider's direction. So . . . he wants to have the honor himself, Raider thought. But to his surprise the Indian reined up his horse and threw his lance into the ground, point first, where it stuck, the shaft vibrating. The Indian slid off his horse and landed lightly on his feet. Hand to hand, then, Raider figured grimly, shifting his grip on the broken portion of the lance tip. However, the Indian made no move toward his own knife. Instead, he held up his empty hand in the universal sign of peace.

"Do you not know me?" he asked Raider in reasonably good English.

Raider let his knife arm drop. Standing erect, he looked more closely at the brave. Yes, underneath the bright lines and curves of the war paint, the Indian did look familiar.

"There were many white men. There was a whip," the Indian said.

Of course! The Indian in Yuma. The one he had saved

from the mob. The one who had later cut the throat of the man who had whipped him.

"You are not our enemy," the Indian said. "Did I not see you being held prisoner by the men with the wagons?"

"Yeah. I was their prisoner."

"You are not our enemy," the Indian repeated. "They are our enemy. Were you there when they shot one of my people?"

"Yes. It was a man called Hendry who did it."

"The one they shot was my brother. He had only fifteen years. He got back to our camp before he died and told us what happened. He is dead now. My brother is dead."

Underneath the flat matter-of-fact voice of the Indian, Raider sensed his grief. And his anger.

"Those evil men must pay," the Indian said simply.

"I'm all for that," Raider said. "But they're getting away."

"They cannot go far with those heavy wagons. Only if they leave them."

"They won't leave them," Raider replied, thinking of the fortune in silver the wagons contained.

The Indian nodded. "The white man is always ready to die for the things he owns."

He looked at Raider for a while. "I am called Standing Bear."

"Raider."

"I salute you, brother."

Damned casual for the middle of a battle, Raider thought, but then, to the Indian, war and battle were more like a game. They spent a good deal of their spare time trying to ambush members of other tribes, sometimes to kill, sometimes not, sometimes to only count coup. A game with occasionally fatal consequences... unless it were a matter of revenge, such as now, and then only the death of the enemy or of oneself would suffice.

Jake's horse, which had run off a ways after its dead rider had fallen from its saddle, was run down and brought back for Raider. Jake's rifle was still in its saddle scabbard. Everyone mounted.

The man Raider had unhorsed laughed and said something in his own language. Other men laughed. Raider didn't know whether he should laugh too.

"He said that you surprised him with your trick with the lance," Standing Bear said.

Raider smiled. "Well, you can tell him he scared the bejesus out of me."

Everyone laughed again when this information had been translated. Then Standing Bear's eyes turned icy. "Now we will kill those men," he said.

But even as they galloped off after the wagons, Raider knew that it was not going to be that easy. The wagons were almost to the hilltop. Once they had formed up, they would have all the advantage. Rifles fired from cover would be proof against any Indian attack, especially over that open ground.

Fortunately, Standing Bear was aware of this too. A couple of his men tried to ride in at the wagons while they were forming up, but heavy gunfire drove them off. One of the Indian's got a bullet through his upper arm. The second had his horse shot out from under him. His wounded companion circled back, lying on the off side of his horse so no more bullets could reach him. His unhorsed companion vaulted up behind him while the horse was going flat out.

Beautiful riding, Raider thought. Give these men the right weapons and a little discipline, instead of the individual bravery thing, and . . . well, Custer had discovered the same thing, but too late.

Standing Bear marshaled his men just out of rifle range. "We will leave them alone for now," he said. "But once it is dark . . ."

Scouts were sent out to keep an eye on the little circle of wagons perched on top of the hill. The rest of the Indians—there were about twenty of them—dismounted and sat together in little groups, laughing and joking, some gambling by throwing small pieces of bone, others eating strips of jerky.

It was already starting to grow dark when a scout came

racing up to the camp on his horse. He slid to the ground while the animal was still moving and rushed up to tell something to Standing Bear.

Standing Bear turned to Raider. "He told me that many white men are coming in this direction from the north."

His eyes were suspicious. Was he going to be cheated of his revenge? Was his quarry about to be rescued?

"They may be friends of mine," Raider said quickly. "Sent for by me to help fight against those men on the hill."

Standing Bear looked at him coolly and for a long time. "Then go and see," he finally said.

Raider quickly mounted Jake's horse and, with the scout for a guide, headed away from the others, all of whom were now quickly mounting in case they had to make a run for it. In most cases Indian's were firm believers in "He who runs away today lives to fight another day." It was not cowardice. It was simply that it was all such a game, and you couldn't play the game if you died needlessly when the odds were too much against you.

In the gathering dusk it was difficult for Raider to make out the identities of the considerable body of men riding toward him. There was one, though, a smallish man, riding a little to one side. The way he sat his horse...

"Doc!" Raider said under his breath.

Raider motioned for his Indian guide to hang back, while he spurred his own mount toward the white men. Doc, recognizing him, rode out to meet him, with another man at his side. As they drew near, Raider saw that the other man was the sheriff from Durango. For the time being, Raider had time only for Doc. "What the hell are you doin' here, you lazy bastard?" he growled, trying to hide his pleasure at seeing his partner. "I figured you'd be somewhere safe in bed, and not alone, neither."

"I have a deathly fear of bed sores," Doc said mildly, also hiding his happiness at seeing his partner alive again. "I'm still a little stiff and sore on one side, but as long as I don't have to do any kind of coarse activity unbecoming a gentleman..."

The sheriff cut in. "What the hell you doin' with that

Indian, Raider? Ute, ain't he?"

"Yeah, he's a Ute," Raider replied. "There's about twenty of 'em down there in the brush, so warn your men not to panic when they see 'em."

"Are those bastards on the warpath agi'n?" the sheriff snarled. "Hell, we'll give 'em a lesson!"

"No, they're *not* on the warpath," Raider snapped. "They're with me. We've got Harrison and Hendry and a bunch of other men and a fortune in stolen silver pinned down about a mile ahead. What the hell's goin' on here, anyhow? Where's McParland?"

Doc cut in before the sheriff could say anything. "McParland sent what men he could round up immediately. I was in Denver, so I came along. The rest of the men are from Durango. A posse. The sheriff here is leading them."

"He's in charge?" Raider asked.

"Damned right I am," the sheriff replied. "I'm gonna git them varmints. Don't need no Indians. They better stay the hell outta my way."

Raider could see greed for the reward money glittering in the sheriff's close-set little eyes. For the time being it would be difficult to reason with him. Raider shrugged. At least they had what appeared to be about twenty fresh men.

"I'll show you where they're holed up," he finally said.

It was fairly dark now, but still, the circle of wagons stood out clearly on its hilltop.

"I'm gonna rush it," the sheriff said nervously.

"You're out of your mind," Raider protested. "They got cover. They'll cut you down."

"We'll be ridin' in outta the dark," the sheriff insisted stubbornly.

"It ain't nowhere near *that* dark."

"Dark enough for me. You comin'?"

"Naw. I'm gonna go over and palaver with the Indians. You comin' with me, Doc?"

"I think I will."

The sheriff snorted derisively, then rounded up his men and began to give them a pep talk.

Doc looked back over his shoulder. "I never did care much for suicide."

"How come he's in charge?"

"A real foul-up from the start. Like I said, McParland was short of men he could use at short notice. . . . Ah, those are your Indian friends, then?"

They were nearing Standing Bear and his men, who waited tensely. Raider quickly reminded Doc of the incident in Arizona, and Doc immediately recognized Standing Bear, even in the dim light.

Standing Bear seemed relieved to see Doc; he recognized him too. "What is happening?" Standing Bear demanded. About a hundred yards away the sheriff was lining up his men.

"You're about to see an exercise in stupidity," Doc said.

"And greed," Raider amended. Sometimes offering a reward had its negative side.

They watched the posse charge the wagon fort, Doc and Raider tense now, the Indians watching impassively. The only thing that saved the majority of the posse members was the growing darkness. Otherwise, most of them would have been killed. As it was, two were killed outright, two horses were lost, and three more men were wounded. None of them made it closer to the wagons than sixty yards. It was the Charge of the Light Brigade all over again on a smaller scale, the wagons erupting with a withering fire, stopping the attack dead, the attackers either falling or milling about, then racing back the way they had come.

Raider and Doc rode out to meet the survivors, who were clustered in a cursing, panting, scared group, looking down at someone lying on the ground. When Raider and Doc swung down from their horses, they saw that it was the sheriff. He'd been shot low down on the right side of his chest. Everyone could hear his punctured lung sucking air through the hole.

Doc had his horse brought up and, taking his medical supplies from his saddlebags, quickly put compresses over both the entrance and exit holes. Fortunately, the bullet had gone all the way through, cleanly.

The sheriff looked blankly up at Doc. "Jesus Christ," he murmured. "Whatta they got in there? An army?"

"No," Doc replied. "Just repeating rifles. The scientific marvel of the modern age."

Raider began giving orders immediately, telling some of the men to fan out in a containing perimeter around the hilltop. The men hesitated, looking numbly down at their fallen leader.

"Do as he says," the sheriff said. "I made a mess outta it, the whole fuckin' thing."

The men, still a little dazed, complied with Raider's orders, but slowly, with a lot of bickering. Finally they moved into their positions.

It was quite a while after full darkness before Raider was satisfied that no one was going to be able to slip through their net. "We'll start sending the Utes in a little later," Raider told the sheriff.

"I don't like usin' Indians against white men," the sheriff wheezed.

"These Indians got the right. Those bastards up on the hill done 'em wrong."

However, the moon came up a short while later, a nice big fat full moon that bathed the entire area in a soft white light. The space in front of the wagons, that brush-clear hundred yards, was a killing ground for anything that moved. There was a little desultory firing back and forth with not much effect. All both sides could do was wait out the night. On the posse's side a good deal of time was devoted to making sure the wounded were as well off as possible. The dead were laid to one side.

Dawn finally came. Some of the posse members had worked their way as far forward into the brush as they could and had either found shelter or had hollowed it out themselves. The lighter it grew, the more the firing increased. Raider heard the familiar deep boom of a Sharps bellowing periodically from the wagons. That was Hendry's gun, the rifle that had brought down the avalanche during the chase through the mountains. Raider had found out that much while he was a captive. One of the posse members had a big single-shot Ballard, which answered the Sharps shot for shot. But this long-range sniping wasn't going to do anyone any good. Especially the defenders behind the wagons. They were pinned down, and a rider had been sent off to Durango to gather more men.

It was time for negotiation. Raider worked his way to a position within shouting range, hoping Hendry's Sharps didn't find him. He called out loudly, "Harrison! It's time we did a little talkin' 'stead o' shootin'!"

No answer. Maybe Harrison had been hit. "Hendry?" Raider called. "Either one o' you. You're trapped. We got more men on the way. Ain't no way to escape. You might as well talk to me."

There was a little more silence, then someone called out from behind the wagons. "They can't talk to you. Ain't neither one of 'em here."

Raider was surprised. "They both been hit?" he asked.

"Uh-uh," came the laconic answer.

Raider thought he recognized the voice as belonging to one of the most intelligent of Harrison's crew. "Well then, why can't they talk?" Raider demanded.

"'Cause they ain't here."

"They ain't *there*?" Raider shouted disbelievingly. "Then where the hell are they?"

"How the hell should I know?" the answer floated back. "The dirty bastards lit out last night before the moon came up. Could be halfway to Mexico by now."

CHAPTER TWENTY

Raider was still stunned by the news of Harrison and Hendry's escape when he heard shouting from behind him. Crawling back out of the range of fire from the wagons, he returned to the rest of the posse. The first person he saw ·vas McParland.

"Well, Raider," he barked. "What the hell is going on?"

McParland had brought another twenty men, all Pinkerton agents. Raider gave McParland the mixed good and bad news—the silver was recovered but the ringleaders of the gang had once again escaped. Or so he'd been told.

"I'll take care of this," McParland said grimly and, to Raider's horror, walked right out into the open. "Hello to the wagons," he bawled.

"For God's sake! They got a Sharps in there," Raider hissed.

McParland gave him a withering glance, then turned back to the front and repeated his call.

"Yeah? Who the hell are you?" a suspicious voice replied from within the circle of wagons.

"James McParland of the Pinkerton National Detective Agency. I want you to throw down your guns."

There was a long silence. "You're really McParland?" the voice from the wagons called out.

"So my mother told me," McParland replied. "Now, I'll give you another five minutes to make up your mind. We've got forty men here and a passel o' Indians. Either you can come on out easy, or we'll dig you out the hard way. Which is it going to be?"

Another long silence, them then a voice saying craftily, "Well . . . this makes things a lot different. We thought you was a buncha bandits, renegades, runnin' around with Indians."

There was some calling back and forth within the wagon fort. The first voice asked, "Hey, Tom, you say you seen McParland before. That look like him?"

"Yeah. Kinda hard to tell at this distance, but that looks like the old walrus."

"The sheriff of Durango's here too," McParland cut in, choosing to ignore the walrus comment. "He's got a hole in him, thanks to you, but he'll live. Now, how about it? You comin' out peaceable?"

"Well, Mr. McParland, we're just honest men doin' our work. We was hired as guards and drivers."

"Then act like honest men. Lay down your weapons and come on out."

Everyone waited tensely. It would be bloody work digging those men out from behind their wooden walls. Finally, a general sigh of relief as the first rifle was chucked out onto the ground outside the wagon circle. More weapons followed.

"Satisfied?" the voice called from behind the wagons.

"Now come on out."

Several of the attackers were in plain view now, their rifles held down at their sides as the first of the defenders stepped out into the open. "How many should there be?" McParland quietly asked Raider.

"Without Hendry and Harrison, nine left alive."

And nine men filed slowly out into the open, one limping,

his pants leg bloody, a couple more showing signs of wounds, but all still on their feet. McParland walked unhurriedly forward, carrying his rifle casually in one hand, as calm as if he were going out for the morning paper. Raider and Doc backed him up, one on either side, their rifles at port arms. The men who had just surrendered shifted their feet nervously, obviously wondering what was going to happen to them.

"Okay, I want to hear about Harrison and Hendry," Raider snapped.

One of the prisoners shrugged. "Not much to tell. Just about the time it got full dark they loaded up a coupla mules with all the silver they could carry and lit out. We thought they was crazy. We'd seen all those fuckin' Indians out there, an' none of us wanted our hair hangin' on some buck's war belt. But I guess they made it, didn't they?"

"Yeah, they made it. You got any explanations, Raider," McParland asked acidly.

Raider came close to blushing. "Well, after the sheriff got shot, it took me a hell of a long time to talk his men into surrounding the hilltop. Harrison and Hendry musta made their break right about then. Moon came out later. No way they'd have made it after that."

McParland looked long and hard at Raider. "Well, at least we got the silver," he said. "Better check out how much they took with them."

Raider, with Doc helping, made a quick inventory of the wagons. One of the first things he found was his .44, in the bottom of a wagon where someone had thrown it. He felt better when he had slipped it back into its holster. His bowie knife was in the same wagon. But there seemed to be one hell of a lot of silver missing. "You say they loaded down two mules," Raider asked the prisoner who'd first told them about Harrison and Hendry's escape.

"Yeah. Two mules," the man said, looking woodenly at Raider.

"Damn! I'd sure as hell like to have a coupla mules like that. I'd make a fortune. Must be the biggest and strongest mules in the whole fuckin' world."

The man said nothing. Raider looked at him suspiciously, then began roaming around the area inside the wagon circle. Right near one of the wagons he discovered what looked like freshly turned earth. "You were diggin' in, I see," Raider said sardonically.

"Uh . . . yeah. We figured it'd be safer."

"Or maybe you were diggin' yourselves a latrine, 'cause it's sure covered up now."

The man looked at him angrily. Raider walked over to a wagon, and, looking inside, he found a shovel. Wordlessly he tossed it to the prisoner and pointed to the ground. Cursing, the prisoner started to dig.

"No, over there," Raider insisted.

Face set, the man dug. He was only down a few inches when the shovel hit something hard.

"That's funny," Raider said. "Don't look like rocky soil to me." He took the shovel away from the man and, scraping away dirt, uncovered several bars of silver.

Doc had come up behind him. "Now, that's what I call a really rich strike. All smelted down and made into convenient bars."

"Yeah," Raider agreed. "Not even Tabor makes strikes like this."

The unwounded prisoners were brought over and ordered to dig up the buried silver. Obviously they had intended coming back to dig it up at some future time when the heat was off.

"A nice try, boys," Doc said, but the prisoners were in no laughing mood.

And then it was time to go after the two escaped leaders. The command was broken up, McParland electing to take the main force and escort the silver and the prisoners back to Denver. Raider and Doc took a dozen men, all of them Pinkertons, and prepared to set out. The Indians were still by themselves several hundred yards away.

Raider, with Doc at his side, rode up to Standing Bear, who was sitting his horse in front of his braves. "We are going after the man who shot your brother," Raider said. "Will you go with us?"

Standing Bear nodded silently, then quickly picked out half a dozen of his warriors, sending the rest back to the main camp.

"Eighteen men with us, counting the Indians," Doc said. "That ought to take care of two fugitives."

"They have a habit of picking up help along the way," Raider replied. Then he signaled, and they began looking for Harrison and Hendry's trail.

The ground around the wagons had by now been pretty thoroughly torn up, so they made a circle to the south but found nothing. The Indians trailed along for a while, then Standing Bear said something to his braves and they scattered. A quarter of an hour later one of them came riding up fast. He and Standing Bear conversed for a moment, and then Standing Bear said to Raider, "They went to the west."

"West? Ain't nothin' out there but desert."

But sure enough, the Indians took them to a little gully a few hundred yards away, and there they found the tracks of two shod horses and two heavily laden mules, heading west.

They followed the tracks for the rest of the day, the white men keeping pretty much together, the Indians fanning out whenever the fugitives' tracks disappeared. About ten miles out, the tracks turned north-northwest and for the next twenty miles continued in that direction.

"Maybe headin' for Utah," Raider muttered to Doc. "Pretty wild country up there. Pretty easy to disappear."

The fugitives were doing their best to hide their tracks. Once they rode their horses up a shallow stream for a mile, leaving the water where the ground was supposedly too hard to show sign, but the Indians found it. Another time they followed along where a small herd of cattle had passed by, trying to lose their tracks among the tracks of the cattle. Later, when a stretch of volcanic scree lay ahead, they had muffled the hooves of their mounts with leather, but still the Indians followed. It all took time, though, and Harrison and Hendry already had a lead of nearly a day.

The landscape grew more and more bizarre as they neared the Colorado. Huge sandstone arches soared overhead. Incredible mazes of twisted sandstone confused their sense of direction. One of the Pinkertons rode up to Doc and Raider. "I come through here a few years back," he said. "Real bad country for the law. Up ahead a ways they call it Robber's Roost. There's a hundred blind canyons to hide out in."

They camped the first night in a well-protected draw. Considering the reputation of the country, guards were posted on rotating shifts all night. They set off again at dawn, the Indians doggedly sniffing out the trail.

Around noon, two distant figures were seen moving perpendicular to the posse's line of direction. "I don't think they saw us," Raider said. "Oh, damn!" Raider added when they were close enough to make out details. "Just a coupla kids."

The men fanned out around the two, a boy and a girl, who were riding mangy-looking nags. The boy was about sixteen and the girl a few years younger, apparently a couple of youngsters just out screwing around. However, when he saw the horsemen, the boy's head jerked around sharply and he laid his hand on the butt of an old rifle that was hanging from his saddle horn. Only when he saw how many men there were did he reluctantly move his hand away from the rifle.

"Let me handle this," Doc said. "You'll scare the hell out of them."

He rode up to the two young people. The boy was sitting his horse easily, slouched a little backwards, but Doc was aware of the animal tension in his wiry young body. The girl looked stupefied. "Good afternoon," Doc said in a friendly voice.

The boy relaxed a little. "Howdy," he drawled.

"My name's Weatherbee."

The boy hesitated. "I'm Butch," he finally said. "Butch Cassidy, from over Circleville way."

The girl giggled. "No he ain't," she said. "He's my cousin, an' his name's Robert LeRoy Parker. He on'y calls hisself Cassidy 'cause he just *worships* that old coot, Mike Cassidy."

The boy flushed. "You just shut your mouth, Annie,"

he snapped. "Mike ain't all that old, an' he's taught me everything I know."

"Well . . . Butch," Doc said. "It's quite a ways from here to Circleville, isn't it?"

The boy shrugged. "I like ridin' down this way. Mike says anybody could hide out here forever."

"It just so happens we're looking for a couple of men who may be hiding out here. Have you seen anyone pass by?"

"You the law?"

"Yes."

The boy's eyes narrowed. "Ain't seen nobody," he snapped.

"Did this Mike Cassidy teach you that, too?"

The boy didn't answer, just wheeled his horse around and rode off. The girl smiled at the men, then rode after her cousin.

"Nasty little brat, ain't he?" Raider said.

"He could be trouble someday," Doc admitted.

The Indians had picked up the trail again. It led to a high plateau. Suddenly the Colorado was far below them, a thousand feet straight down, a sheer drop. They followed the river east for a ways, looking for a route that would take them down and across it. About five miles farther along Raider spotted something obviously man-made on the edge of the cliff overlooking the river. It looked like a huge clay jar, half buried in the cliff. There was a hole at the top.

Standing Bear saw it too. "It is of the Anasazi," he said. "It was made to put corn inside, or so I have been told."

"Those old buggers really got around, didn't they?" Raider said to Doc.

Another mile farther along a huge rock jutted out into space above the river. Doc insisted on dismounting and walking out onto the rock.

"Doc, how the hell can you do that?" Raider demanded, his stomach heaving as he stared down at the sheer drop below.

"The view, Raider. The view."

Soon after that the cliff began to descend in height and

they found a way down to the river. They made camp on a sandy little beach. There was nothing in evidence around them but wilderness. It was immensely peaceful, so peaceful that it was hard to believe they were hunting down men who would kill them if given the chance. And whom they might have to kill.

Harrison and Hendry's trail picked up again on the other side of the ford. The way led through very broken country. Finally, what appeared to be a solid wall of rock loomed ahead of them. However, the fugitives' tracks led them to a narrow fissure running from top to bottom of the mass of rock. There was room for only one horseman at a time to enter.

"I don't like the looks of this," Raider murmured.

Neither did the Indians. "Very dangerous," Standing Bear said.

Nevertheless, the posse continued in single file, Raider in the lead. He felt claustrophobic. Bare rock walls rose hundreds of feet straight up on either side of him. He doubted there was room to turn a horse. His skin crawled. One man ahead with a rifle . . .

They met that man with the rifle a half hour later. Raider had just rounded a turn in the passage through the rock. A straight stretch lay ahead, then another turn with a ledge above it. The only thing that saved him was that he saw a ray of sunlight reflect off the barrel of the man's rifle. Raider quickly hauled on the reins, trying to get his horse to turn. The animal couldn't; it reared, then sidestepped, which spoiled the rifleman's aim. His first shot spanged off the rock walls and went ricocheting off behind Raider, nearly hitting Doc. Raider had to slide out of the saddle and guide his horse backwards. Another shot came, this one thudding into his saddle, fortunately now empty.

He got his horse back around the corner and managed to turn him, but even though he and the others were out of sight of the rifleman ahead, they were not yet out of danger. The man kept firing, and the bullets ricocheted around the corner, buzzing among the men. One cried out, his arm creased.

"Get the hell back," Raider shouted.

The men, bunched up and cursing, managed to get their animals under control, and they all hightailed it out of range of any more ricochets.

Panting, Raider looked over at Doc. "Well, we ain't gonna get any further up that way, are we?"

CHAPTER TWENTY-ONE

"Harrison . . . Hendry," Raider called out. "Maybe we can't get in to you, but you sure as hell ain't gonna get out. Give yourselves up."

A mocking laugh came bouncing back down the stone passageway. "Go to hell, lawman."

"That's not Harrison's voice," Doc said.

"It ain't Hendry neither. The bastards've gone and done it again. Found someone to help 'em."

"I imagine having two mule loads of silver with them didn't hurt. I wonder how many . . .?"

"All it takes is one or two, the way this place is built. I wish we had a map, but I kinda think there ain't never been one made."

"Maybe it's a complete dead end."

"I can't see them two boys going into anything they can't get out of. Maybe I can get 'em to talk a little."

Raider eased himself closer to the bend in the stone passageway. "Hey! You up there! I wanna talk to Harrison or Hendry."

Once again the laughter boomed back down toward them. "No way, buddy. Them two birds are guests in our little hotel. Payin' guests, an' we don't like our guests bein' disturbed. 'Specially by no-good sneakin', lyin', spyin' Pinkertons, an' I got me a hunch that's just what you are."

"They don't seem to appreciate the efforts we make to bring law and order to this tortured land," Doc said morosely. "I think—"

"Raider," Standing Bear's voice cut in. "One of my people knows something of this place." The Indian was standing next to his horse a few yards away.

"Is there another way in?" Raider demanded.

"Perhaps. We ourselves do not know. We do know that on the far side of this narrow passageway lies the land of an Indian people. We do not understand what white men are doing there. Perhaps if we look for those who rightfully belong there..."

Raider and Doc pondered for a while. "It's a long shot," Raider finally said, "but what the hell other choice we got?"

Two men were left behind in the rock passageway to make certain that no one left by that route. Guarded by armed men, it was equally impassable in either direction. The rest of the posse rode back out into the open. A camp was made while Standing Bear's braves rode off in various directions.

It was late at night before they began returning. One man came riding up, another Indian riding alongside him, an Indian Raider had not seen before and, from his dress and general appearance, obviously of a different tribe. Standing Bear immediately went over to the newcomer. A lengthy conversation followed. Finally, Standing Bear approached Doc and Raider.

"It is as I thought," he told them. He pointed to the Indian who had just arrived. "This man's tribe lived in a small valley behind the stone passageway. There are not many of them, but they have lived there since before the time of their fathers' fathers' fathers. Then, several seasons ago, a few white men came and, by treachery, forced the tribe to leave the valley. Now those white men use the valley of the tribe, and they use it for evil things. Many evil white men come there: killers, robbers, white men who are running away from the white man's law. They feel safe in the valley."

"But is there another way in?" Raider asked tensely.

"The man says yes. It is a carefully hidden way and a difficult one, but easier to pass through than the one ahead of us now. It is a secret way protected by the tribe for generations, but he has told me he will show us the way in if we promise to make those white man go away forever from their land."

"Oh, they'll go away all right," Raider said grimly.

Standing Bear nodded his head, his face expressionless. "I believe you," he said.

It was decided to ride through the night. The Indian promised them they would be able to enter the valley just before dawn, taking by surprise the small band of outlaws who were now so arrogantly controlling it.

It was a very difficult ride, over rough, broken country. There were ridges to cross and deep sandy gullies to traverse. Fortunately the moon was nearly full, making the journey easier. Its frosty light turned the bizarre landscape into a magic land. Long shadows stretched away from high rock towers. There was enough light from the moon to see the layers of banded rock patterning the buttes and columns, but only the pattern. The moonlight showed no color.

The little cavalcade was passing through a deep canyon with smooth walls of rock rising on either side when Raider suddenly noticed a strange and threatening figure looming over him. "Jesus!" he snarled, jerking his horse to the side. Then he saw that what had startled him was only the odd, stylized figure of a man painted onto the smooth rock. Doc rode over, his curiosity whetted. The Indians hung back. "Anasazi," Raider heard one of them mutter.

"They're really quite beautiful, in a primitive way," Doc said quietly. Most of the figures were bulky and only slightly humanoid, but some were slender and graceful. "The tree of life," Doc said, pointing to a representation of a small tree sprouting from the fingers of one figure.

Standing Bear rode closer. He looked at the paintings

for quite a while, unmoving. Then he said, "It is a good sign. We will be successful. The Old Ones are with us."

They rode on. Finally, just before dawn, the Indian guides motioned for everyone to be silent. "The way down into the valley is just ahead," the Indian from the valley said. "They have a guard at the head of the trail."

"Damn," Raider murmured. "If he gives us away..."

The Indian drew a long knife from his belt. "He is one of the men who drove us from our valley," he said. "I will see that he gives us no trouble."

Before Raider could say anything, the Indian had slipped away into the darkness. Raider had a glimpse of him going down onto his belly and slithering toward the trail head. He moved absolutely noiselessly, and then he was gone. Long minutes passed. Raider and Doc thought they heard boots scrambling against gravel, then a choking sound, but they couldn't be certain. About five minutes later the Indian came back, wiping the blade of his knife. "There was only one guard," he said calmly, his eyes glowing.

The posse rode slowly past the dead body of the guard, indistinct in the poor light, a large dark pool soaking into the ground on each side of his throat. "Gives me the creeps," one of the white posse members muttered. "Don't like ridin' with Indians."

"Beats ridin' against 'em," another man put in.

The way down was very difficult. At several points the men had to dismount and lead their horses. It was gradually growing lighter. There was considerable danger they would be discovered before they made it all the way down. They'd be sitting ducks, jammed helplessly together on the narrow path which ran down the steep side of the valley.

It was now light enough to see the valley itself. It was very beautiful, about two miles long by a half-mile wide, the bottom of it mostly flat, with a stream running near the side on which the posse were descending. Small stands of trees dotted the valley floor. There was a little cluster of Indian dwellings and white men's shacks just a couple of hundred yards on the other side of the stream. A thin column of smoke was rising from the roof of one of the shacks. Someone was already up.

Finally the posse made it behind the shoulder of a low outcropping near the base of the trail. Here they were sheltered from view. Now it was time to wait. Raider had ordered the two men left behind at the bottleneck in the rock passage to create a diversion, which Raider figured would be coming up soon.

Raider could see the entrance to that rock passage. It was a shallow V on the far side of the valley. He thought he could see a man on guard where the V met the rock. He checked his watch. It was time. Suddenly, on cue, a racket of firing came from the rock passage, amplified and echoing because of the rock but still far away. There was a lot of firing; he'd given orders to burn ammunition as if the whole force was attacking. He could hear the guard firing back.

Nothing happened down below for a few seconds, then men began running out of the buildings and heading toward the rock passage, guns in hand. Raider counted ten men. He waited until they were halfway across the open space that led to the rock passage, all of them on foot. Then he gave the word. "In at the charge!" he bellowed. "Ride around 'em and cut 'em off!"

His little command burst out of its hiding place, the white men shouting, the Indians whooping shrilly. The men below didn't notice them for a moment, then abruptly stopped running and looked wildly around them. Some tried to run for the shelter of the rock passage in spite of all the firing taking place there, others headed toward a stand of trees, and others dropped onto the ground and began firing at the charging posse.

They didn't stand a chance. One wing of the posse swept around them, cutting the men off from the shelter of the rock passage, killing most of those running in that direction. The group heading for the trees was cut down almost to a man. Only those lying on the ground firing back held the attackers off for any length of time, and then they were overwhelmed by the charging riders.

One small group of attackers made for the houses, to check if any of the outlaws were hiding there. They had ridden up close to the shack showing the smoke when a middle-aged woman wearing ragged, dirty clothing stepped out of the shack, screaming curses from a nearly toothless mouth. She held a shotgun and she was raising it, but the man she was aiming at hesitated because he had never shot at a woman before. He hesitated too long—the woman blew him out of the saddle. Cursing, his partner put a bullet through the woman's head.

Doc galloped down the small row of buildings. He saw a man leading a horse out of a small barn. It was Harrison. "Drop the reins!" Doc shouted.

Harrison spun around, pulled a pistol from his belt, and snapped off a shot at Doc. Doc leveled his Winchester and fired back, working the lever rapidly, sending a storm of bullets Harrison's way. He saw Harrison wince, and his left arm went limp. Then Harrison was running toward one of the buildings, still firing with his pistol. Doc's bullets kicked up dust all around him, and then the rifle was empty.

Doc cursed. He had no more ammunition for the Winchester. Most of the men carried both rifle and pistol in .44-.40 caliber, so that they would interchangeably take the same ammunition, but Doc still had the .38 Lightning. Well, maybe a pistol would be more useful inside a building anyhow.

He swung down from his horse and ran over to the house. It was the largest structure in the valley, consisting of several rooms. He tried peering around the corner of a doorframe, and a bullet splintered the wood next to his head. Harrison was in there, all right, and shooting quite well, as usual.

No choice but to go in after him. But how? Doc quickly looked around and saw that a large bedroll was lying next to the door. He bent down and picked it up. It was fairly heavy. Pausing next to the door, he stuck his pistol in his belt and, taking a deep breath, threw the bedroll into the room, way to one side. A shot immediately rang out. Harrison had fired at the bedroll. And then Doc was inside the door, crouching next to the doorframe, pistol in hand.

Harrison was standing near the back wall, his left arm hanging uselessly. He saw Doc immediately and swung his pistol in Doc's direction. Both he and Doc fired at the same instant, and both missed. But because Doc's pistol was a double-action and Harrison had to recock his pistol each time he fired, Doc's second shot was a fraction of a second faster. He put a bullet into Harrison's body. Harrison flinched, and his shot went wild. Doc kept firing, pumping bullet after bullet into Harrison, but the man wouldn't go down. Doc was beginning to understand Raider's criticism of the hitting power of his .38. Then Doc's pistol was empty— amazingly fast—and he realized he'd just put six rounds right into the middle of his target. And Harrison was still standing.

Harrison had managed to fire back once, missing again, and now he staggered forward, hunched in pain, and brought his pistol into line with Doc once again. Cursing, Doc ducked back through the doorway, frantically fumbling in his pocket for more shells. A bullet followed him out.

Doc crouched behind a water barrel, furiously shucking out empties and stuffing in live shells. He was halfway finished when Harrison appeared in the doorway, weaving from side to side. His eyes tracked around and locked onto Doc. Doc abandoned his reloading efforts, ready to make do with the two or three live rounds he had in the cylinder. Then he realized he wasn't going to need them. Harrison was trying to bring his gun up, but he wasn't succeeding. Doc watched the wounded man's fingers loosen around the butt, and then the pistol thudded to the ground. Harrison took one shambling step forward, coughed blood, and fell heavily. Doc looked down at Harrison's body, then at his .38. "Took you long enough," he snarled at the gun.

Meanwhile, Raider was racing over the valley floor, directing his men in mopping up the outlaws. More than half of the defenders were down, either dead or wounded. The remainder had thrown down their weapons and were begging for mercy.

Standing Bear was riding beside Raider. "This man, Hendry," the Indian demanded. "Is he one of these?"

Raider had made a survey of the dead, the wounded, and the prisoners. "No, damn it," he said. "I hope the bastard hasn't lit out again."

And then he saw movement farther down the valley, just a single glimpse of something disappearing around a clump of brush. It could have been a man, it could have been an animal fleeing the noise and confusion, but it was definitely worth checking out.

It was Hendry. Raider was able to recognize his lumbering way of moving even from several hundred yards away. He apparently still believed he hadn't been seen, and he was trotting along, low to the ground, heading for the far end of the valley.

Standing Bear had seen him too. "Is that the one?" he asked. Raider nodded. "Then he is mine," the Indian said softly.

He nudged his horse into a trot, then into a canter. Finally into a run. Hendry didn't hear the approaching rider until Standing Bear was only a hundred yards away. Pehaps the softer sound of the Indian pony's unshod hooves hadn't been noticeable. Then Hendry turned and saw the Indian bearing down on him. Hendry tripped and almost went down. Then, turning and steadying himself, he began firing at Standing Bear with his revolver.

Standing Bear made a difficult target. He was weaving his horse from side to side, lying low along the animal's neck. Nevertheless, Raider, riding a little way behind, saw a red streak of blood suddenly appear on the Indian's back. One of Hendry's bullets had at least grazed him.

And then Standing Bear was on Hendry. Raider saw the lance raised, heard Hendry scream in fear, start to turn and run—and then the lance flashed down. Raider could clearly hear the heavy thud as it slammed into and through Hendry's chest, slightly from one side, transfixing him at an angle.

Hendry staggered back, staring down in horror at the lance shaft jutting from his body. He slowly settled down onto his knees while Standing Bear rode in a small circle, cantering up to Hendry. Indian and white man looked at one another, then Hendry's gaze dropped to the lance again.

He wrapped both hands around the blood-slippery shaft and tried to pull it out, then screamed horribly. He fell forward, the leverage of the lance shaft turning him slightly to one side. Raider could see the bloody tip jutting from his back. Hendry jerked a couple of times, and then it was all over.

Raider rode over to Standing Bear. The Indian was looking down expressionlessly at the dead man. Both Raider and Standing Bear remained silent. Then, to Raider's amazement, he heard the sound of distant singing. Looking up, he saw a long line of people and horses moving down the trail into the valley.

Standing Bear looked up too, his eyes gleaming. "The people are coming back to their valley," he said quietly. He looked down at Hendry, then back up at the descending Indians, and although he said nothing, Raider thought he understood what Standing Bear was thinking.

The Indians had come out ahead this time.

CHAPTER TWENTY-TWO

Raider tugged desperately at the tight, chafing collar of his boiled shirt. "Doc," he hissed. "Do I look as silly as I feel?"

Doc gave his partner an amused examination. A picture of uncomfortable elegance from head to foot: frock coat, striped banker's pants, white spats, low-heeled shoes polished to a high gloss, high wing collar, boiler-plate starched shirtfront, vest, and a look of agony on his wind and sun-burned outdoorsman's face.

Doc himself felt right at home in identical garb. "Look!" he suddenly said to Raider. "It's the President!"

"President o' what?" Raider asked sullenly, trying to look without turning his head. His shirt collar rubbed his neck every time he moved.

"President of the United States," Doc snapped. "Chester A. Arthur himself. Hell, maybe you even voted for him."

"I don't vote. Far as I'm concerned, all politicians are thieves. I don't want to feel guilty for helpin' put 'em in office."

"Well, that aside, it's something to have the President here."

"Don't matter to me. He's here to see Tabor and Baby Doe, not us."

"Ah yes, Baby Doe. Isn't she lovely," Doc murmured as he watched that young woman hold out her hand to the President to be kissed. "What a gown she's wearing. I heard it cost over seven thousand dollars."

"Doc," Raider sighed. "Sometimes you sound just like some little old lady. It's only a wedding, even if the President of the United States is here and the groom is loaded with money."

It was nearly three months after the Harrison-Hendry gang had been wiped out and Tabor's missing silver recovered. The setting was the stately Willard Hotel in Washington, D. C. Tabor had finally realized his dream of becoming a United States senator, but alas, he had not won the Big Casino. He had been hoping for the full six-year term, but the messiness of his personal life had intruded. On January 2, 1883, his long-suffering wife, Augusta, had finally filed for divorce. It had been a sensational case, with Tabor and Baby Doe cast as the villains. Augusta pitiably proclaimed to the court—and to the newspapers—that divorce was the last thing she really wanted.

The whole thing surfaced just as the Colorada legislature was in the act of choosing its senators. Tabor had previously been a shoo-in for the six-year term, but not even a frontier state was going to elect a public debauchee as its national representative. Someone else got the six-year term; Tabor was awarded the remaining thirty days of Henry Teller's unexpired term.

Hurt at first, Tabor shrugged off his disappointment and immediately left for Washington, determined to have a ball. Many of the solons in the august halls of the Senate were appalled at the apparent crudeness of this self-made silver Croesus, but they were all quite eager to enjoy his hospitality. More than once a crucial Senate vote was delayed because Senator Tabor from Colorado had the men with the key votes out for a drink.

Tabor brought Baby Doe to Washington at the end of his term. Grateful for what Doc and Raider had done for him, he invited them to the wedding. Not only the President attended, but also the entire Colorado congressional delegation, including Henry Teller, Nathaniel Hill, Jerome Chaffee, and Judge James Belford. However, the First Lady was not in attendance, nor were the virtuous wives of the distinguished senators and congressmen. Baby Doe was too far beyond the pale.

"Hey, who are those two people?" Raider asked Doc, jerking his chin in the direction of an elderly couple who were wandering around the elegant room in a semi-daze.

"The McCourts from Oshkosh," Doc replied. "The parents of the bride."

"Well, I'll be . . . Guess they never thought their little girl would make it so big. God, look at her—rich as hell and beautiful on top of it. Lucky bastard, Tabor. Lucky woman. Damned lucky, both of 'em."

Doc glanced over at Raider, an odd expression on his face. "Careful," he said softly. "Don't tempt the gods, Raider."

EPILOGUE

Doc's warning to Raider was genuinely prescient. The Tabors, H. A. W. and Baby Doe, lived like royalty for another ten years: private railway coaches, mansions, platoons of servants, different-colored coaches for different days of the week—everything that money could buy. And then in 1893 the price of silver plummeted. Overnight, Tabor was wiped out. In a dozen years he'd run through $42 million, a sucker for any investment scheme proposed to him, no matter what its merits. Now, to his bewilderment, he was bankrupt.

Friends in Colorado secured for him an appointment as postmaster of Denver. He held the position until he died in 1899. After that, there was nothing left. All Tabor had been able to hold on to was the Matchless Mine, now totally played out. Tabor's last words to his wife were "Hold on to the Matchless."

Baby Doe proved to be as faithful to her husband after his death as she had been during his life. For thirty-five years she lived in a shack above the Matchless, dressed in rags, with burlap wrapped around her feet, living off charity.

The walls of her shack were covered with faded newspaper clippings recounting her past glories.

Finally, on the morning of March 7, 1935, Baby Doe was found dead in her shack. The Lady of Leadville had frozen to death during the night.

Sic transit gloria mundi.